About the Author

Sinead Flynn is from the West of Ireland, she started writing her first novel "*Superwoman*" in 2014. Having been an avid reader all her life, it was always an ambition of hers to write a book herself. Sinead enjoys reading, *Eastenders* and Twitter.

Dedication

This book is dedicated to Michael, my parents, all my sisters, nieces and nephews and both my dogs.

Sinead Flynn

SUPERWOMAN

AUSTIN MACAULEY
PUBLISHERS LTD.

Copyright © Sinead Flynn (2016)

The right of Sinead Flynn to be identified as author of this work has been asserted by her in accordance with section 77 and 78 of the Copyright, Designs and Patents Act 1988.

All rights reserved. No part of this publication may be reproduced, stored in a retrieval system, or transmitted in any form or by any means, electronic, mechanical, photocopying, recording, or otherwise, without the prior permission of the publishers.

Any person who commits any unauthorized act in relation to this publication may be liable to criminal prosecution and civil claims for damages.

A CIP catalogue record for this title is available from the British Library.

ISBN 9781784557775 (Paperback)
ISBN 9781784557782 (Hardback)
ISBN 9781784557799 (E-Book)

www.austinmacauley.com

First Published (2016)
Austin Macauley Publishers Ltd.
25 Canada Square
Canary Wharf
London
E14 5LQ

Chapter 1

I hustled down the quays at 4.45 on a Monday morning, yawning and lashing back strong coffee from the flimsy cardboard cup that was uniform for my entire ilk at this time. The fog mist and hazy rain depressed Dublin city as it had all January.

Hurried and late as usual I was attempting that sort of half paced hobble-run that you will often see be-heeled women sport. I use the word 'attempt' loosely as it usually ends with the woman mortified in a heap, covered in tea as one heel has decided to skid in a manner that would put Torvil and Dean to shame.

I was hasty as I was supposed to be meeting workmates at Heuston station at 4.30 to catch the airport bus. We were due in Edinburgh at 9.00, which meant a flight at the company's expense, hence the early morning cheapo plane tickets.

I was only going so I could type, copy and fetch coffees, I thought it childish mutiny, and I could do that in fucking Dublin. I don't enjoy early mornings. Who does?

I especially don't enjoy freezing cold, drizzly mornings. Even an entire forty minute bus journey away, I could hear my bed calling me. Since starting my working life, I had learned a very good lesson about never undermining the value of sleep ... and vodka.

In all the furore and hustle, I barely noticed that someone had caught my elbow; this was strange on two counts:

1) The only reason someone would have stopped me, is to tell me that I had dropped something in my haste. This was mad, but nice enough. Unheard of though, because in a city that can be so anonymous and a bit ... rough, you could drop your box of babies behind you and nobody would let you know. What if they had to like ... engage in conversation?!

2) In most cities, touching someone you don't know is considered so weird, overfamiliar, creepy and impolite, that it's akin to suddenly deciding to rest your testicles on them for a bit.

You can imagine my surprise I'm sure, when I realised that the elbow holder appeared to be steering me towards and into a lane-way. You know the sort, cobbled, bookended by large buildings that were shops, flats and other things, like launderettes. I flicked my head around to see what was going on. I saw a man; he looked young, mid-twenties I'd bet. He also had a nice coat. For all the days I would remember this morning, I'd never forget this coat.

I'd seen it in the men's section of Zara two weeks previously and was jealous and annoyed that there was no female counterpart. I'd considered buying it even so, but it was just that bit too swampy. It was gorgeous though, all lovely chestnut leather brown, with woollen pleated cuffs.

It's okay, I thought, men with nice coats from Zara don't steer you down lanes. I must have been a bit slow from the early morning, because that's exactly what he did. The next thing that I actually remember is being beside a huge wheelie bin, down the lane.

It was then that I saw the syringe in his hand.

Fear shot through me and I tried to push past him in escape, no luck. I was pushed by the chest, forcefully until I hit the wall behind me. My head clunked against it and my vision spun. I slipped to the ground, dizzy and trying to shy away. I felt myself being pulled back up. I heard him speak, but I was too stunned to hear words, just an aggressive harsh tone. He took my bag, then after pulling at my pockets, he found my phone and took that, too. After waving the syringe at me again, he told me to stay where I was and not to move, or else ... something ... I can't remember.

People who have been mugged will tell you of their horror and icy cold fear that froze them to the spot rendering them incapable of defending themselves. Most people, (myself included), would say "Ah no, I have a plan you see, if I got mugged, I'd jab the bastard with my keys, or spray my deodorant in his eyes, or kick him in the unmentionables (Balls). I was guilty of this myself, well, I can tell you with the benefit of hindsight, that they're right. You really do become incapable and useless at defending yourself. I just stood there, useless, like a bloody chocolate teapot, or a priest at a brothel.

He was gone in seconds; I watched his back as he tore away, back into the street.

I decided then that it would be okay to breath. I hadn't the whole time he was there. My breath came in huge gasps, yet I didn't catch one of them. I was heaving and yelping for air, but I couldn't breathe.

A woman appeared – I suppose she heard me. Now that I look back, I can imagine her discomfort at finding a grown woman, sobbing, snotty-nosed, and hysterical for oxygen, down a lane.

The woman garnered the story from me I think, though I couldn't tell you what I said. Guards arrived, and after I had repeated the story to them, I was placed in their car, trembling and quivering like a four-year-old.

I remember the guard in the passenger seat trying to make conversation with me, the one driving didn't bother. I couldn't find the words to reply to him, so after a while he gave up.

We arrived at the building where I lived. I exited the car and looked up to the third floor of the old Georgian building. Quickly, I scurried up the steps to my large red front door; nearly stoned on the familiarity and safeness of home.

I then realised that I didn't have keys, so I rang the buzzer.

"Yeah?" came my flatmate Amanda's answer.

"Amanda, open the door, it's Louise ... and the guards," I replied.

The intercom went dead, and shortly after, the door was swung open. Embarrassingly enough, this wasn't the first time I'd been delivered to her by the rozzers, and we'd only been flatmates for six months. See, I'd overdone it at a friend's birthday bash in town. The newest, hottest nightclub was the chosen venue and free booze was the tool of choice to fool everyone into thinking they had had a great time. I'm sure you know the kind of place, a "Vibrant" (mental) DJ, who spoke nonsense over the songs; half naked promo girls peddling shots. The kind of girls who make you decided that you're definitely going on the "I'm a celebrity, get me out of here" diet of beans, rice and the occasional crocodiles anus … tomorrow, after your kebab.

Anyway, I never made it to kebab o'clock and was brought home by the temple bar five – oh after thinking they were a taxi and trying to hail them. I still made them stop for chips though.

Amanda looked worried and confused when she surveyed me and the two coppers, at the door. I had been worried that she would be annoyed at their presence, owing to her habit of trying to grow magic mushrooms in the bathroom. It was different this time though, I was a victim, and she could piss off for herself. I was overwhelmed with relief to see her though, a friendly face and the smell of home. I stepped inside with the urgency that someone getting off the Titanic might have.

The guards filled Amanda in on my ordeal, and she ferried me into our flat and into my bedroom. I was touched by her concern and felt like being mothered, so I let her. Not that I had any objections to going back to bed, delighted so I was! Or would have been, if I wasn't so sad.

In my room, I walked past the mirror, well, I didn't have much choice, my bedroom was so small that if you bent over, your bum touched the window and your head hit the wall, you'd get wedged. I was not a pretty sight. My crying had resulted in panda eyes, blotchy skin and a shiny red nose that would put a sixty-year-old alcoholic to shame. My forehead had a graze, and my chin. I had only noticed the cuts and scrapes on my hands and knees before then; they stung, and now so did my head. Where I had banged it off the wall was the worst. Gingerly, I prodded it with my finger, and winced at the pain. I checked my hand, and noticed some blood.

"Christ, I better ring a doctor," said Amanda.

"Yeah, please, the guards said I had to anyways, for evidence or something. They wanted to bring me to the hospital, but I couldn't face it, not on my own." To my shame, my eyes started to water again, my lip quivered, and I burst into fresh tears.

Amanda swooped on me and gently pulled me into a hug.

"Shh, now babes, it'll be alright, you're home now, you're grand," she soothed.

"I'm ... huhh ... sorry," I cried, mortified by my sobs.

"Don't be silly! You poor thing, it must have been awful, come on, get into your pyjamas and stuff, and I'll make you some tea, and then ring the doctor," said Amanda firmly, as she left the room.

When Amanda returned, with hot drinks and toast, I was strangely relieved to see her.

"I just realised, this calls for a sick day, I've already called your work, and told them you wouldn't be going to Edinburgh," she informed me.

Amanda flopped on my bed, after first placing cups and plates on my bedside locker, I was too traumatised to chastise her about coasters.

"This is great," beamed Amanda, then she looked appalled at herself.

"Not you getting robbed, of course, but hey! No work! On a Monday! And that's the shittest day! Auld cranky arse Biggins said I've to get a sick cert, this is my third since Christmas, but I'll get the doctor to write it when he gets here. Delighted that I didn't get dressed, all day to faff around in our jammys!" she cheered. I smiled back weakly and grimaced and the headache I was starting to get.

I didn't blame her though, Amanda worked at the social welfare, denying peoples claims and catching them water skiing when their supposed to be paraplegic. I think that's what she does anyway. She doesn't seem to like it very much and harbours a burning dream to run away to a cruise ship to be an entertainer.

Unkind people might describe her as weird, or a hippy, or a bit mad. In fairness, she doesn't help this with her appearance. Amanda is beautiful, but has white blonde, curly hair, that sometimes has rainbow streaks that she matches with tutus and the like. She even sometimes, and this is hard to say about my own flatmate and friend, wears coloured mascara and a little flower in her hair … to work – in an office. I heard her auntie pulled in some favours to get her the job.

I, on the other hand, find her warm, caring and kind, a great flatmate, and well able to down a mixture of Ouzo, Cointreau and vodka, and that's a true story.

Chapter 2

Sometime later, still nestled in my bed with Amanda at my side, curled like a kitten, basking in her sick day glory, I noticed that she was chattering on. I nodded along, but didn't feel part of the conversation, detached somehow. I kept feeling as though I was being dragged back to that lane way. I couldn't stop thinking about it; I wasn't even thinking anything specific about it. I was stuck in the terror, it burned inside me and I fought the urge to hyperventilate. I tried to shake it off, but Amanda looked at me strangely, and I realised how odd it must look.

The buzzer went off, indicating the arrival of the good doctor. Amanda got up to let him in, and a short while later, he entered my bedroom, all business with his bag.

"So, Louise, you've had a shock, pet, haven't you?" He smiled kindly, and I noted our first name terms, probably from my frequent phone calls to get sick certs for Amanda.

"I'm fine really, just some cuts and scrapes, my heads a bit banged up as well, the Guards are insisting that I get a medical report though," I explained pragmatically, eager for him to know that it wasn't really my fault that he was here, at half seven on a Monday morning. I hoped he would go easy on me.

With the intimacy of a long-term lover, he examined me, then cleaned my cuts and put a small stitch on the worst one, on my knee. His attention turned to my head, he asked all the questions you might expect about nausea, dizziness and headaches, and deemed my poor battered head as "Fine, but you won't be doing any raving for a while, heh heh heh!"

Thanks a bunch ... I thought.

After he had finished stitching and poking, he suggested a mild sedative and wrote a prescription. I relaxed at the thought of getting something to rid me of the underlying, troubling, impending doom sort of feeling. The trouble with impending doom was that I'd already had my bit of doom, so I was alright. It was very confusing, this shock malarkey. I'd have my lovely sedative soon though, and then I'd be grand, I decided.

After the doctor had left, Amanda offered to get dressed and visit the twenty-four chemists for the Tranqs. I was very grateful, the twenty-four-hour chemist was ages away, and usually full of dodgy-looking people and teenage boys buying condoms. But the other, nice, clean, friendly chemist wouldn't be open for two hours. I didn't offer to go myself, I didn't fancy heading out with my poor old head, leaving my bedroom that had duvets and Sky HD. I also noted that the uneasy feeling got worse when I contemplated going outside, having said that, it was still on 8 a.m., so I was still pretty shook up. 8 a.m. How had so much time passed?

Although I hadn't been able to concentrate while she was talking, I missed Amanda as soon as she left. I chain smoked, and when I wasn't smoking, I bit my nails and contemplated mad, scary things. Amanda was taking too long, the chemist wasn't *that* far away, she had been gone a good thirty minutes.

I then experienced blinding fear that she had been attacked, or knocked down by a car, or something equally awful. Terrible things could happen to someone outdoors, things that had never concerned me before. The threat of busy roads and seemingly horrible strangers that inhabited the word seemed luminous in my mind.

When I heard her key in the door after another twenty minutes, I was practically climbing the walls. I breathed a sigh of relief so deep that I went into a coughing fit. It might have been the thirteen cigarettes, but we'll say it was relief.

"What kept you so long? You were gone nearly an hour!" I bellowed to the hall, with an almost accusing tone.

"I went to the shop and the DVD place, to get provisions!" She looked bewildered. In what I think was an attempt to calm me, Amanda produced carrier bags, revealing fags, pastries, sweets and rom-coms. Not forgetting, of course, the small white tablets of serenity that the Doctor had given.

"The price of those!" She gestured to the tablets.

"Oh sorry, how much do I owe you? I'll give you some cash later, I'm a bit short at the minute," I replied, then started to laugh maniacally.

I ripped open the packet and swallowed the first of my tablets with the dregs of a bottle of warm flat coke. I wondered how long they would take to work.

I settled back in the pillows and waiting for the bliss to come, everyone knows sedatives are great.

A friend of mine had been on Xanax for a while and she described it as "A bit like being stoned off your head, but without the paranoia or the urge to eat baked bean sandwiches and laugh at everything." I'll have that please, thanks very much.

Amanda passed her phone to me, "I know you're ... upset, but you should ring the bank and credit card people and probably your parents ... that's what the guards said anyways, well, not about your parents but the other things," she explained.

Bless her, she hated to put pressure on people. Her instinct to mind me battled with the sense of duty that was somewhere, deep down in her. She really was a great friend, and flatmate.

I did have my reservations about the new tenant that the landlord had given me. I had grown used to having the place to myself after the Korean Chap had left, six months previously. After speaking to Amanda on the phone, and warning her about Mrs Upstairs, I braced myself for when she came to view her room.

I had childishly planned to plant dead fish behind the radiator, tell tales of ghosts, and ask her to join my Satanist cult, all in the name of scaring her off. When she told me about her encounter with Mrs Upstairs though, I knew I had met a kindred spirit.

Let me explain, Mrs Upstairs, also known as Marie, or Liz, or something like that, was a cow. She was about sixtyish, and looked like she worked in a government department, like taxation or sewage, something not nice anyways. She wore thick chunky corded jumpers and twee little twinsets to work, looking all the part of a little old lady She was impolite, complained to us about things that she had clearly made up, yelled at us for leaving post in the communal hallway or if we played music.

The omens of their friendship were never good; I had warned Amanda about her on the phone, hoping to put her off. When they did meet, Mrs Upstairs, sensing movement, propelled herself into the landing.

"Is it Louise you're looking for? That's number three, don't be banging too loud, although you might have to, she has that music so loud," she bitched.

Amanda quickly cottoned on that this was the neighbour that I had told her about and when I opened my door I found Amanda patting a furious Mrs Upstairs on the head, and telling her she was a "Good dog". Mrs Upstairs has become much worse since, but I've never regretted Amanda moving in.

Chapter 3

After long exhausting phone calls with various banks and other official type people that left me grinding my teeth at the idiocy of people who worked in customer service, I decided to go for broke, misery wise, and call my parents.

It may be clichéd, but I, like most women my age, dreaded calling my parents, I liked them, loved them to death, but god, a phone call with them was the most stressful twenty minutes of anyone's day.

I would love to have one of those bohemian types "we're all adults, now let's drink wine and discuss intellectual matters" relationships with my parents. But I was Irish, it didn't work like that. I had the sort of relationship that meant that I rang them once a week, heard inconsequential local gossip from my mother, and asked my dad questions about fixing my toaster.

I searched Dad's number on Amanda's phone and rang.

"HELLO?" boomed Mam's voice. "Hello? Can you hear me? IS IT ON?!"

"Mam? Hi, It's Louise, yes, the phones on, stop shouting," I replied, rolling my eyes like a surly fourteen-year-old.

"Wait, why do you have Dad's phone?" I asked. This was unusual, Dad always had his phone. As an insurance sales man, his company had gifted him an iPhone for work purposes. I had hoped that Dad would pass on the message to Mam. I didn't like to be the bearer of bad news to her, my mother could be easily worried.

"Oh, well, c'mere till I tell you, I'm after finding this game, it's called floppy bird, and its brilliant. It's terrible easy, but I can't get past ten points. Oh, while I have you, what's a Wi-Fi?

I keeps asking me to connect to it? She pronounced it "Wiffy", "I really must start those computer classes," she said and I couldn't help but smile at my mother's techno naivety.

"It's like the internet, Mam, don't mind it. The thing is, I've a bit of bad news," I said, a pause ensued, and I swear I could feel her anxiety through the phone.

"Right, emm, well, I had a bit of trouble this morning, someone took my bag and phone and things on the way to the airport, I'm fine though!" I hastened to add. I felt awful for burdening her with this, I was old enough to look after myself. Although I knew if she found out from someone else she would brain me, and never let me forget it. At least I didn't have to tell her about the syringe, and the shoving, toning it down for Mam actually made it seem less drastic for me, weirdly enough.

"Mary mother o' god! Are you okay?! Are you at home? I'll get your father to go collect you, he's on his way! Is the robber there now? Call the police!" She was shrill, and spoke all in one breath.

"I'm grand," I sighed. "The Guards have been and gone and the doctor, there's not a bother on me, no need to send Dad, so *relax*," I ordered firmly.

"I'll ring your father, and see what he thinks of all this," she replied suspiciously, as if I was lying about my welfare and was secretly dead.

"Is Amanda with you? Tell her I was asking for her." Mam seemed to calm quite quickly, I was jealous of her resilience.

"Yeah she is, she says hello. Look, there's no need to ring Dad at work, besides, you have his phone," I replied. I was regretting this call; I think she was making me worse.

"He has my phone; I made him swap for the day so I could get the hang of flippy bird," said Mam. Poor old Dad, using Mam's ancient blokia for the day.

"Alright, I'll let you ring him so, I've to go, I'm on Amanda's credit, talk soon, love you, byyee." I was desperate to end the call, the panic was reaching nail-biting point again, I couldn't even smoke because Mam would hear, and sadly enough, she still didn't know that I was a smoker.

"No, wait, you ring him, its better from you, he'll only worry if he doesn't speak to you," said Mam, with an anxious tone.

"Right, okay, bye." I rolled my eyes, frustrated by her indecisiveness.

I hung up and caught Amanda looking at me, worry on her face, "What's wrong with you? Was your mam worried?"

"No, I just remembered about my mother's ability to drive me up the wall from hundreds of miles away," I explained, then felt guilty, Mam only cared.

Ten minutes later, I had repeated the same PG version of the story to him, I much preferred the story that I told my parents to what actually happened. Dad also offered his services to drive from Kilkenny to Dublin to bring me to our home town, Lacknamon.

"I'm fine, honestly, Dad, look after Mam, she sounded a bit stressed after I told her, I was trying to get you first actually, I hate telling her things like this," I said.

"She's grand," Dad dismissed. "She just gets worried about you, all on your own in Dublin. You should have stayed in Lacknamon, there are no muggers here, and at least we would be able to keep an auld eye on you." He repeated the age old argument, in which Lacknamon was portrayed as a veritable Eden of serenity.

He couldn't fool me though, I'd been there, done that, got the small town parochial T-shirt.

"Yes, Dad, but I've decided to break family tradition and live more than three feet from my parental home," I said, making a childish barb at my sister, I wasn't in the mood to defend my actions to anyone right now, besides the pills were making a tad dopey, I could feel the brain fog descending and I wanted to be allowed to enjoy it.

After Dad rang off, Amanda looked at me with a glint in her eye. "Wait till I tell you about yer man from the video shop, he asked me to go out with him on Friday night!" She looked triumphant, I didn't blame her, and we had been discussing him and his potential rideability for months at length.

"No way! I was incredulous and almost choked on the pastry that I was devouring. "I hope you fuckin' said yes!" Although strangely, I was already getting nervous about spending Friday night alone. Stoppit, I told myself, the shock will be well gone by then, and I certainly didn't intend on getting any more socks, they were rubbish. The pills were nice though.

"*OF course* I did," she exclaimed. "He's taking me bowling," she grimaced. "I know, its crap and boring and I'll have to wear the smelly shoes, but if I go to the cinema I'll feel obliged to let him pick the film, I can't sit through another boring heejit film about guns, tits and explosions, their even worse!" she whined.

"On your head be it, although I don't know why you won't just go for a bite to eat with him, these teenagery dates are all good and well, but it seems like a young woman's game to me," I yawned.

"No, what if we sit down and have nothing to talk about? I'd die of disappointment, he's so lovely-looking, I don't think I could take two hours of sitting in silence, at least we'll be distracted with bowling," she reasoned.

I nodded along in agreement, but I starting to feel more and more heavy, in a nice way, the way you get after getting into warm clothes after being drenched in rain. The panic was still there, but it was further away from me – a safe distance.

I decided it was reasonably safe to watch a chick flick with Amanda and maybe a few Malteasers wouldn't do me any harm either. I fell asleep five minutes in, it was just 10 a.m.

Chapter 4

I feel a bit duped. Here I am, telling you all about being robbed and going a bit funny from it, but you barely know me. So before I keep going I'll tell you a few things about myself and I'll try and make it quick and painless and not too boring, go on, humour me.

My name, is Louise Casey, I'm twenty-six, and I work as an administrator for a company called DPL accounts. I don't have anything to do with accounts though, even though I've worked there for three years. They offered to train me up a bit, even offered to pay for it, but I said no. This job is just a stop gap until I decide on my 'forever' job. I still don't know what that's going to be, I just know that it has to get better than typing up useless reports and filing. I'd rather become a bin man for Osama Bin Laden than become an accountant, I've seen them at it, the accountants, and its looks boring as fuck.

I live with Amanda, and she's lovely, and I have lots of acquaintances, people I know I mean, but really only a handful of friends. There's Alison, who I've known since we were tiny, we actually both wet ourselves at an unforgettable production of the nativity scene when we were four. Since then, we've stopped wetting ourselves, but kept the synchronicity. Anywhere we've been, we tend to go together. We've worked in promotions, for nightclubs mainly. Getting twisted on free booze and pretending to like people so they would actually visit the club paying us. We still describe it as the best days of our lives. Alison would still be at it if we let her, however, she impressed everyone by getting a job as a bar manager, it pays better apparently (it would want to), and she gets to be mean to rude people by ignoring them at the bar. A powerful job in Ireland, trust me.

Alison is what my mother would describe as a "Wild woman", although my mother also once described her as "A brazen wagon." In fairness to mam though, Alison had just puked on her flower beds, aged fifteen, and having tried vodka for the first time.

Alison is fast-paced, always keeps herself occupied, chain smokes, and is loyal well past the point of fisticuffs. She, unlike me, has millions of friends – I've made her promise that I'm her favourite though. The phrase 'party animal' was invented for her, and I do most of my going out on her orders. It was actually her birthday that the cops brought me home from. Alison's married to Tony, a freelance insurance sales person who is loaded. I once asked her to tell me how much money he had, and she just winked conspiratorially. Though maybe he's not as loaded as he once was, since the recession, less people want insurance, seeing as most of them are losing the homes they wanted to insure in the first place. Either way, they seem to have a nice time together, and since they let me be maid of honour, I've forgiven them for getting married and making me look a spinster.

Any other friends I have are kind of non-descript, we see each other occasionally: normally at birthdays, christenings and the like and exchange gossip on Facebook, like Lorna, who used to work at DPL, a total star, a really good friend, but I just can't be arsed keeping up with her life, and I know she feels the same about me, so we keep in touch, but its low maintenance.

I have just one sibling, a sister called Annie, she has two kids and an incredibly intelligent husband called Brian who works doing something involving hard maths, nobody really knows what it is. Annie is a great sister, a great daughter, a great mother, and a great wife. She had a habit of trying to be everything to everyone and generally gets steamrollered in the process. She wasn't always such a saint, we never let her forget the days when she was partying and tormenting us all by "Acting the pure maggot" (my mother's words). One famous tale in our family folklore was the time she fell asleep on her way home from the pub, on a swing in a children's play park, she spent all night there, woke up frozen to the bone with a hangover that would "knock a donkey sideways". The walk home, apparently, included school children laughing, parents looking at her like she was "the next Fred West" and a good puke behind a Nissan Sunny. I only remind her of this when she won't let me smoke in her house, or when she won't lend me something, usually clothes.

Annie weighs about three stone and has one of those figures that supermodels are killing themselves for. Not a bingo wing, stretch mark of jiggly thigh in sight, despite being mother to two. I've always lamented the unfairness of this, because she actually eats more than those people on embarrassing bodies, where Dr. Christian puts all the food they've eaten in one week onto a big table in an attempt to shame them skinny, but they just look lustily at the food, and he looks like a right knob head.

Annie's two children, my nephews, are great. Callum is fourteen and is doing his Goth phase. He carries about an air of gloom and indifference but soon lights up and beams through his shaggy emo fringe when the play station is mentioned. Callum was born when I was only twelve, which meant that I got all the babysitting jobs as a teenager. This has led to a nice little bond between us, and I like to think of myself as his confidante, this is what I like to think, but for all I know, he could think I am as "gay" and "crap" as he tells his parents he thinks about them. It's all just teenage hormones though, and even though he thinks I'm ancient, he's sympathetic to my plight and shows me how to use my phone.

Oscar, Annie's other son, is six and I'm his godmother. I asked her why she waited so long between children and she told me that she had only just finished cleaning the house and catching up on sleep from Callum's terrible twos.

Oscar didn't seem to go through these turbulent times and he's honestly the funniest person I've ever met. He calls me his fairy godmother and buys me perfume at Christmas. When I visit, he takes me to collect insects in the garden with him and his dearest ambition is to find a radioactive spider to bite him and give him superpowers.

Annie ended her wild youth by getting pregnant at seventeen, then the erratic, spontaneous party girl that she was, changed into a grown up, got engaged, then married (a year and a bit later) to Brian. Her "Baby daddy" as I called him to annoy her.

My parents, Sarah and Patrick I think they're called, are typical Irish culchies. Dad works at the Credit Union, and Mam minds the house. Dad sorts the bills, and she does the washing. They are the nightmare of the feminist movement, but the thing is, if Mam woke up tomorrow and decided to get all empowered and start taking control, Dad would be fine with it. He's always just done things to make her happy, he minds her and she idolises him for it. They restore my faith in love and romance, when I've been out with a series of arseholes and need cheering up.

I've no boyfriend, but it's okay, I don't want one for the minute. That's not to say that I wouldn't be delighted if say, Ryan Reynolds, came knocking. But I'm worn out after the last one. Kevin was a lovely guy, but drove me mad with his constant *niceness*. He was always buying me flowers and chocolates and all that shite men think women want. He even watched *The Notebook* and declared *Twilight* to be a masterpiece. He was more womanly than I am.

This turned out to be true when I broke up with him. He made a show of us in a coffee shop by crying and saying he'd do anything. He then turned rather nasty, called me a bitch through his spiky, watery eyelashes and stormed off yelling that I'd die alone because I was cold and didn't know a good man when I had one, Charming. He also left me to pay the bill. Funnily enough, it was actually the most attracted I'd been to him in months; though I've always been most interested in men who treat me like shite, repulsed by the lovely ones. Sods law it seems.

Emmm, I've no other people really. Apart from work people and they don't count, but I'll tell you anyways. It's a massive company with branches all over the world, but the Dublin branch has only about thirty staff. There's no office banter to speak of, but we do a lotto syndicate (which I've never won, not once, in three years ... not that I'm bitter). I think the accountants go out for pints at the weekend, but they don't invite us lowly admin staff.

Our boss is more elusive than Santa Claus and I've only seen him once, at my job interview, he even left halfway through to take a call. He seems very busy and we don't mind, because if he's harassing someone else, then he's leaving us alone. We call him Mr Fawlty, because that's his name. See? No banter.

Aside from that I have a lovely flat. I've lived in it for two years after a succession of absolute kips, and although am only renting it, I've painted and decorated and even installed things like kitchen counters. My friends all thought I was mad, for they were normal renters, unable to commit to even buying a new kettle for fear of moving and losing their money. I have such a compulsion to make it lovely though, it's my pride and joy and I'm more likely to spend my last twenty quid on a new lamp than a new lipstick, though I actually spend far too much on both.

So that's that over with, now we can get on with the proper business of you hearing all about me, going round the twist.

Chapter 5

A long time later, I woke to the sound of the TV booming out the *EastEnders* theme tune. There was an awful pain in my right hip. I dragged my eyes open, feeling very confused. Eyes open, I found myself on the couch, the pain in my hip was Amanda's foot in my kidneys. I remembered all that had happened that morning and was suddenly crushed by despair. The urge to hide under the duvet and go back to sleep was only out burned by how awful I felt.

Physically, my limbs weighed about a tonne and were stiff. My eyelids were sleep-filled, my eyes watered as I yawned so deeply that I nearly gave myself lockjaw. Aside from that, I felt that I had an emotional vodka hangover. The type you get when you wake up beside a traffic cone, still in your disco clothes, a bag of peas on your throbbing ankle and no memory. Terrifying.

As potent as it felt, I didn't understand my fear, hence my confusion. I was safe, at home. I hadn't drank in well over a week, so there was no booze induced depression. Or the beer fear as it's known.

Amanda was awake, and she smiled widely at me.

"You're awake, about time, it's nearly ten in the night, I recorded the soaps for you, I did try and wake you up, but you mumbled something about how I could fuck off for myself, so I left you for a bit," she grinned cheekily.

"I'm alright, the pills are a bit strong, I'm a bit ropey to be honest." I sat up, it cost me the effort of a thousand chin-ups, but I did it.

I noticed the empty sweet wrappers littering the room when I was groping around for cigarettes, normally I would be looking for leftovers, but I the queasy heat had returned to my stomach and I wasn't able for food at all.

A red-haired harridan was screeching on the TV in a cockney brogue, I fought the urge to fling something at the TV, I normally loved this show, I must have been really tired and irritable I decided.

I returned to sleep after about a thousand more cigarettes. I remember Amanda telling me that Alison had called, and thinking that I'd call her back in a minute, just as I sank into oblivion again.

The next time I woke, I was alone. This really freaked me out, I knew where I was, but the room was dark, and my eyes hadn't adjusted to it so I could see nothing. Stress rose in the chest, like an iron ball, threatening to choke me. I followed the blinky light of the TV on standby and stumbled over to turn it on. The room filled with a bluish light, illuminating the mess in the living room.

I relaxed for a moment, slightly, though I held a stance like a ninja in combat. Then I decided, no, not good enough. The light went on, and so the kitchen fluorescent. I made myself tea, like a good little Irish person, and as I walked to the living room, still disturbed by my earlier reaction, I got the urge to run, as though there was something nasty behind me, following me. I tried to hold onto rationality, but ended up power walking back to the sofa, glancing over my shoulder.

I flicked through the TV, looking for distraction. However, it was 3 a.m., and all I could find was sitcom repeats and adverts for magic hoovers. The sitcoms went on, and I found them oddly comforting. I hoped to lose myself in undemanding cheesy pie American telly until I could relax and find sleep again, because, unbelievably, I was still *so* tired.

I spent the whole night like this. On the occasions where I found myself drifting off, I shot back awake, like a gaoler, caught sleeping on the job. Something in me told me to keep the light on, even though it was burning my eyes. I wouldn't allow myself to go to bed, as I didn't fancy being stalked through the hall by my imagination again.

When daylight broke, I decided to it was safe to move around the flat again. Somehow the light pouring through the windows made everything less eerie. At a loose end, I had a fit of the Pollyanna's and decided to make Amanda's breakfast. A full fry-up I decided, even though she normally just had coffee and fags whilst running around half dressed, looking for a jumper or tights or whatever.

I forced some perk into my steps as I slapped sausages and bacon into the pan, a short while later, I jumped when I heard Amanda's voice behind me.

"Oh it's you, I thought the flat was on fire, what's that arsey smell?" she asked.

Then I noticed my blunder, food normally had to be taken out of its plastic packaging before being cooked. I stood at the cooker, confused by my brain fart.

"Breakfasts off!" I chirped at Amanda.

"Good, food makes me gawk in the morning," she replied, while opening the window to let out the burnt plastic smell.

"Erm, sit down," said Amanda, "you been awake long? You look awful, no offense," she added quickly.

"Yeah, I've been up a while," I replied, secretive about my weirdly spent night.

"Seriously, you look dog rough, maybe you should see about another day off?" she asked, sounding wistful, and maybe, a tiny bit jealous?

"Yeah, will you ring in dead for me? God, I'll be sacked," I groused.

Taking two consecutive days off in DPL was tantamount to introducing naked Tuesday to the office.

"Feck them, you haven't had a sick day in months, you deserve a good mitch, especially after yesterday." Amanda always reckons that I work too much, and is appalled by the amount of lackey work I get left with by the senior administrators.

While Amanda called the office, I hid in the sitting room, too fearful to listen. The idea of having to go outdoors and face work was grim to contemplate.

When she came to me, she looked bewildered and said, "You're off ... till Monday, paid and everything, lucky cow!" She looked surprised though and I was too. I nearly fell off my chair with astonishment, when my grandmother passes away, I had practically had to beg for the day off for the funeral, and was made to work late all week to make up for it.

"Who did you speak to?" I asked, sceptically. I was worried that this was a practical joke by an intern on a power trip.

"Mr Fawlty himself, would you believe? He sounded like he just wanted to get rid of me to be honest," she groused, clearly unimpressed.

"Right, fuck this, I'm going to bed, have a good day ... Look after yourself," I added, in case she didn't know.

"Aww, I'm so jealous," whined Amanda. "If my head fell off in the morning I'd still be expected to put in an appearance," complained Amanda. "I need coffee," she said, and then rambled off to the kitchen.

Warily I went off to my bedroom, still shaken by sinister night I had experienced. Once in my room, I closed the curtains, barring the daylight, which taunted me and seemed to scold me for the fruitless day ahead of me.

I took the next tablet on the small blister pad that Amanda had brought from the chemist, and waited for unconsciousness to fetch me.

Chapter 6

Three days later, I was no better. I followed the pattern that I had unknowingly started on Monday: sleeping all day and sitting awake all night, flitting from one room to the night, like some kind of lunatic night watchman.

The only difference was that I had run out of those golden pills that the doctor had given me. So when I say that I slept all day I mean that I dozed, fitful and light. Without the stimulation of the tablets, which I suspected from the off were sleeping pills, I found it impossible to sleep, and dreamt of horrible masked men, pulling me in all directions. The dreams were so vivid that I could smell their breath, horrid and warm against my face as I struggled against their grasp.

The strangers in my dreams, yelled with distorted voices about wanting something, but wouldn't specify what. I could neither see nor feel my surroundings, only dark violent shoves. When I woke up, I would sob and fight for breath, covered in sweat and feeling as though my skeleton would shake from my body.

The pills ran out two days ago, and I had seriously considered visiting the doctor for more, because I knew they would help. When it came to getting dressed and actually doing so, my motivation abandoned me. Actually doing something of purpose became my Everest.

I was tired beyond belief all the time; it wasn't just my nocturnal lifestyle that was exhausting me either. I couldn't get out of my own head, thoughts and worries were dragged to the forefront of my mind and they sat their immovable and insurmountable. Distraction, which had been a useful tool until now, no longer worked, TV couldn't hold my attention and left my hands to wander. My nails were in bits from my constant chewing. I tried to read a book, only to find myself, half an hour later, staring into space fighting horrible intrusive thoughts.

Despite my macabre mind-set, I was still hopeful that this plague of semi-comatose terror would pass. I don't know whether it was laziness or sense, but I decided it was pointless visiting the doctor, I'd be better soon; I had to be, because this was unbearable.

Amanda had clearly noticed something amiss; she had heard me sprinting through the flat on the second night after the mugging. Clearly concerned, she offered to sit up with me, but I couldn't let her, as much as I had wanted to. She had work and even in my distress, I couldn't let myself be that selfish.

I felt guilty enough as it was, it can't have been nice for Amanda, living with me. On the rare occasions that I noticed her speaking to me, I was distracted and uncommunicative, unable to be enthusiastic in a conversation. I had locked myself in my own little isolation station.

Amanda came home from work to find the answering machine full of messages from my parents, my sister Alison, even a short one from Kevin, saying he couldn't get hold of me at work and was I avoiding him? (I was); although I was avoiding everyone, but for different reasons obviously. I was too embarrassed by my current state of my mind. I had even put Amanda in an impossible position by asking her not to tell anyone. I knew I would only get a reprieve for so long, and that when Monday came I would be back at work and normal service would resume. I'd be better by then, I repeated, like a mantra. I just need a few days, and then I'll be better.

Friday passed, sleep infused with occasional bursts of panic and the perpetual feeling of imminent disaster. When Amanda came home from work and started to get ready for her date that I remembered I would be home alone tonight. Possibly all night if it went well. How could I manage the whole night without the security of another person's presence? I tried not to wake Amanda at night; nevertheless, I still needed to know she was there.

I considered asking her to stay in, and then was awash with guilt for even considering it. She had been so excited all week and deserved the night off after becoming my nursemaid and PA all week; Fielding phone calls and making dinners that were left uneaten.

I'll be fine; I thought repeatedly, I'll keep busy. I wasn't convinced.

How had I become this needy, outrageously dependent person? What was happening to my mind? Was this a descent into madness? I didn't know, and was becoming anxious that I would never again be the person I was.

Amanda looked great as she left for the night, if a little bizarre in a chiffon skirt with a flowery cardigan. I sometimes tried to get her to dress down for dates, but those dates never went any better than the ones when she was just herself, so I let her be these days.

"I would say don't wait up, but I know you will. If I do pull tonight, I'll be home as early as I can in the morning, ring me if you need me, and I'll come home." She looked so worried, the guilt nearly floored me. I assured her in a clipped, no nonsense voice, like a bossy matron, that I would be fine, and basically threw her out the door.

Uneventful hours passed and I remained as calm as I could. Huddled on the sofa I drank tea, smoked, tried to eat, and managed a whole slice of toast. In the middle of recorded *Who Wants to Be a Millionaire*, my worst fear was realised. A huge crash came from behind my bedroom door. Fear zipped through me like electricity and I froze, paralysed with fright. There was someone in the flat, in my bedroom, all my nightmares came alive at once. I edged towards the room and still there was crashes, bangs, the sound of stuff being thrown around emanating from inside.

I ran from the flat like an Olympic sprinter; stopping only at the bottom of the stairs. I then lost all reason and screamed blue murder for help. I heard footsteps on the stairs above me and nearly passed out with dread. Was this an attacker?

I noticed Mikhal, our neighbour, standing at the top of the stairs. I noticed his kindly eyes and the stricken expression on his face. And explained about the noise, in my garbled, hysterical own way. Mrs Upstairs then joined us. She arrived giving out stink about the noise, but changed her tune when she saw Mikhal, I've always reckoned she fancied him. I supposed he could be her type, for an older woman anyways. I put him at around sixty. Polish and very quiet, I liked to think he was an artist; he had a very soulful look, like he spent hours every day, painting and pondering the meaning of life and that sort of thing.

Mikhal beckoned me upstairs and I went, trembling. Then he dodged behind his own front door and retrieved an umbrella. If this was his weapon of choice, it certainly didn't inspire much confidence. Mikhal strode into my flat, looking as menacing as someone can with an umbrella that was covered in little yellow stars.

Mikhal was gone ages, and I began to worry that he had been overpowered. Mrs Upstairs and I considered calling for the guards, but as we were doing so, Mikhal exited my flat.

"I think you forget kitten?" he asked, delicately with a thick polish inflection.

"No, I don't have a cat, a *kitten?* In my flat? Are you sure? He opened his cupped hands to show a small ginger thing, obviously the kitten in question." *Shit*, he must have come through the window," I answered, quietly, puce with embarrassment.

Mrs Upstairs started on about the landlord not allowing pets, clearly she thought I was lying and had forgotten about the pet cat I kept in my room, like you do. She skulked off, tutting and wittering on. The bitch.

When she had gone, Mikhal subtly double-checked that it really wasn't my kitten, then ushered me into my flat. "No worry, I will find home for little cat, you're fine now, yes?" he asked

"Yes, thanks so much, you're very good." Now that the shock had worn off, I was feeling immensely foolish and was keen to disappear behind my door. I didn't want to seem ungrateful though, so I waited for him to walk away before going back inside.

Around an hour later, Amanda arrived home, just as I was starting my *Dr. Who* marathon. I'd begun to record things for night time. I may have been losing my mind, but I didn't want to miss all the good telly.

"Mrs Upstairs just went ballistic at me, apparently you have a cat and you woke up the whole building? Is she making it up and do you really have a cat?" She looked excited.

"I don't have a feckin' cat," I groaned with embarrassment. I confessed what had happened to Amanda, and she nearly pissed herself laughing. This did not help with the awful burning shamely shame I felt, but it was nice to make her laugh after the week I had given her. Also, the fact that she was back so early didn't bode well for the success of her date.

"Good night?" I asked, casually, not wanting to make a big deal about it.

Amanda rolled her eyes, sighed dramatically, plonked cross-legged on the end of the couch and launched into her story.

It had gone well it transpired, at first. They went bowling and had such a fantastic time that they went for a drink afterwards. Then several drinks later, they had gotten to the snogging in the taxi stage. It was when they arrived at his place that the trouble started. It seemed, video shop man had a bit of a thing about Mel Gibson, and his home was a shrine to the fact. Not just a poster here and there, Amanda jeered, with disgust on her face, but actual life-sized cardboard cutouts of Mel Gibson dotted around the place. When Amanda visited the bathroom, looking for a chance to regain her composure, she was greeted by Mel on the back of the door, in *Braveheart*, rocking his kilt and blue face paint.

"How do these loopers manage to hide it so well? I thought he was normal, well I certainly didn't think he was that fucking nuts, anyways," she lamented.

Apparently my fragile state had come in useful when she faked a text saying that I was unwell and legged it out the door and into the taxi before he had had a chance to suggest the watched *Passion of the Christ* as foreplay.

"And the worst thing is, now we'll have to rent DVDs from somewhere else, all the way into town we'll have to go!" exclaimed Amanda, like someone short-changed on *Watchdog*.

"Anyways, I'm going to bed, unless you want me to wait up with you?" she asked, considerate, even though she was a bit jarred.

I declined, she had made this offer every night, but I was better off seeing the night though alone, no point in us both losing sleep.

"Goodnight, get some sleep, you'll need it for the morning, you'll be dying." I knew full well she'd sleep in tomorrow, like every other normal person on a Saturday morning.

Chapter 7

Monday morning and I was at the front door, in my big girl clothes for work. The previous night had been the worst of my entire life. I was so anxious about needing sleep to be on top form for work that I made myself stay awake all day fighting the urge to drop off, only to find myself revving up when I tried to sleep that night. I spent the whole night tossing and turning, and eventually gave myself a neck cramp trying to find comfort.

I tried everything: a soothing shower, which I badly needed anyways, gacky camomile tea, counting sheep, even tried to read myself tired and got three quarters of the way through the latest Harry Potter though my concentration was shot. I was desperate, frustrated and generally in the horrors. At five in the morning, I gave up and returned to my post of biting my nails in front of the TV. As a result of my early morning, I got ready miles too early, which is just as well, as I needed the time to cover my battle scars. I looked in the mirror for the first time all week and reeled at my reflection. I looked like me, but worse, which is saying something. I've never been mad about my appearance anyways, but after a week of being left to its own devices, my looks hadn't improved. My usually waxed eyebrows had grown alarmingly bushy, like an old mans, my skin was blotched and dotted with millions of blackheads from smoking. I also noticed that my skin had turned a funny grey/green colour, except for the dark circles under my eyes.

I had allowed my hair to dry naturally last night, because I couldn't be arsed to blow dry it. The resulted in to spreading outwards in frizz, like a big brown yield sign.

"Amanda! I've a head, like a bag of mince, and stupid hair and I've to go to work!" I shrieked to the kitchen, where she was necking caffeine.

She strode into the bathroom, "Well, I wasn't going to say, but, well, fuck it, it's only work," she consoled to no avail.

I looked like Father Jack Hackett.

We larded on the makeup and straighted the bejaysus out of my hair. After the seventh (and I'm not exaggerating) layer of concealer, had been applied, we admitted defeat, and decided that my worrying appearance would help with the sympathy vote when I got bollocked for being out all week.

I threw down cup after cup of coffee, trying to stimulate myself into motivation. As I left, she checked me, like a mother to a six-year-old, "Got your handbag? Keys? Phone?" she asked.

The only reason I had these things was because Amanda had sorted them, getting keys cut, pulling out old handbags, and even rooting out an old mobile for me.

It was the first day of school all over again and I yearned to cling to her leg and beg to be allowed to stay home and watch cartoons.

Leaving the flat was like doing a bungee jump, I knew that if I thought too much, then I'd never do it, the fear would take over and I would go back to cowering on the couch.

So I grabbed my coat, and my second favourite handbag, (that bastard had robbed my good Chloe one), and propelled myself out the door. What I didn't expect was the outside world to be such a sensory overload. After living indoors like a hermit for a full week, I was blown away by the hustle of a busy city. Y forced bravado that had gotten me as far as the path promptly abandoned me. The daylight was astoundingly strong and the traffic deafened me. Angry workers beeped their horns, they were stuck in a very long tail back and they were very vocal about their displeasure to say the least. I was glad I didn't have this problem, I didn't drive. Although this meant that I relied on public transport to get around, I was still glad. Driving in this city was expensive, with insurance, parking, petrol, the whole lot, it was a rob. It also didn't help that my attempts at learning to drive went ... not great.

I can do this, I told myself, I've been walking to the bus stop for years, and once again I swallowed the fear and stepped into the throng.

I never noticed how fast people walked before. They zigzagged around me, when I couldn't keep the pace and I definitely heard someone muttering about "Fuckin' culchies" when they bruised past me in their hurries.

I made it to the bus stop, and after the customary forty minute wait, the promises of sacrifices to Satan and the gift of forty virgins had been made to the bus company, the bus arrived. It was heaving with people, like those trains you see on the telly in India. I stepped on, half expecting to see livestock and people playing drums, but it was just the usual flock of miserable bastards on their way to work. A man followed me onto the bus, where had to stand, squashed against a dozen others and wafted his bag of what I can only assume was garlic and vomit around, so everyone could experience the aroma. Then he nestled his arse cheeks either side of my thigh or had proceeded to have a good fart for himself.

The bus lurched forward and everyone did the usual comedy skid forwards on the wet, yet somehow still sticky floor. Apart from the smug gobshites that held the handrails who looked self-satisfied, still upright without and general debris all up their back. They might think themselves clever, but I wouldn't touch those rails if I was paid a million euro, having frequently witnessed people picking their nose then grabbing them.

Our first stop prompted the departure of a thousand or so school children, who ram raided the exit and didn't seem happy until they had pushed everyone a few inches closer together, I swear I felt garlic vomit man's colon on my knee.

After twenty minutes of this hell, I felt my bag vibrate, and then heard my phone ring.

I answered.

"Hey, its Amanda, c'mere, one of the girls from your work was just here, she said not to go in, and she left a letter for you?" questioned Amanda.

"Which girl? Who?" I said, almost accusingly in my confusion.

"Erm ... Maire I think?"

The office Manager, not good, it was probably my P45.

"Open it, see what it says?" A strong sense of foreboding came across me. Whatever this was, I knew it wasn't good. It was never going to be "Hey, you've won a million euros, take a week off work and go on the lash."

I heard letter opening noises, paper tearing, a page unfolding, and then a pause whilst Amanda read on.

"Come home, you need to read this yourself I think," said Amanda, awkwardly.

"Ah, just tell me! What is it?" I half whispered, not wanting the other passengers on the bus to overhear.

"Right ... ermm ... I'll read it to you," Amanda said, uncertainly.

I half listened whilst she rattled off the letter, I wasn't really surprised, the usual "It is with deep regret that we must inform you of the closure of our branch in Dublin" ... wait ... what? Was I fired?

"What?" I asked, incredulously.

"Yeah, their closing down the whole place, apparently it's to do with the 'current financial climate'," answered Amanda.

"Oh," I replied, dumbstruck.

Selfishly, I thought, well at least it wasn't just me. Then I had the good grace to be ashamed of myself. I was lucky enough, I was young, single, had no dependants. There were people in that office that had kids, mortgages, and sick mothers in nursing homes.

"Oh god, that's awful, are you okay, Louise?" asked Amanda, delicately.

"Yeah ... right, I'll be home in bit, see you soon," I managed.

"Erm ... I've to go to work," replied Amanda, tensely, clearly mortified to be so lucky.

"Yeah, of course, I'll see you tonight then, bye," I said, then hung up.

I exhaled deeply and my shoulders slumped. I hadn't even realised how tightly tensed they were. I was, of course, worried about my unemployment and that of my former colleagues and the economy and all that, but ... well, I couldn't help but feel relieved. I could go home, guilt free.

It was then I realised why they had given me all last week off, it was to soften the blow. Come to think of it, there had been a lot of lateness ignored recently. Even the management had been kinder to us lowly peasants in admin, coffees were bought, cakes and sweets seemed to be bountiful. It was almost like the last day of school when the teacher hands out loads of sweets, regardless of the E numbers, because the kids aren't her problem anymore.

In the midst of this bought of generosity, there had been an underlying sinister tone. Things like photocopiers, expensive machinery, and more worryingly, staff members had begun to disappear quietly in the night.

I couldn't believe that I hadn't seen it coming. We had shag all business these days. A lot of the staff were bored, making work up out of nothing for themselves. We had numerous pep talks about hard work prevailing and productivity improving. The people in charge of bringing in new clients were looking greyer by the day, Greyer still when they realised that the astronomical budget they were usually assigned for lavish restaurants and golf club meetings was being sliced in half.

However, we had all thought that we were *safe,* we worked for a huge multinational, and they had tonnes of money – goes to show.

I noticed an empty seat on the bus and took it, noting that I was actually getting further and further from home, where I now wanted to go. I waited for the next stop and when it came I jumped off, not without thanking the driver first.

I'm not sure what I was thanking him for exactly, overcrowding the bus? Slamming the breaks every three seconds? Or perhaps booming reggae music through the radio, enhancing the third world ambiance on the rickety, smelly tin can they called a bus? But, I was Irish, and for some reason that meant I felt like a snobbish heel if I didn't say thanks.

Miraculously quickly, my bus home arrived. Even better, I got a seat. After expecting a working day, going home at this time was really disorientating. Sitting on the bus I was almost cheerful, without work I could now go home and … what exactly?

The realisation that I was now task-less struck me. Was the foreseeable future going to be a repeat of last week? Would I become a free-floating gypsy of the apartment? Nothing to do and my whole life to do it. And how the fuck would I pay my rent?

The weight of the enormity of losing my job crushed me suddenly. To my mortification, I found that I was hyperventilating. Other passengers averted their gaze while I looked around. I didn't blame them, it was always best to avoid the looper on the bus. The poor unfortunate who had enthusiastically plonked himself beside me earlier was clearly regretting his decision, and actually moved seats.

I couldn't believe the state of me. I was roaring, crying, gasping and losing all control in public. It was bad enough at home, but to have an audience made it a hundred times worse.

The quiet, soft-spoken people, whom I had shared the bus with quite contentedly, seemed scary and menacing now. Teenagers on their way to school became thugs before my eyes. The bus swerved dangerously close to another car and I let out an involuntary yelp of shock and fear. I had convinced myself that the other passengers were out to get me and the driver was trying to kill us all.

By now, I was really drawing a crowd. The other passengers exchanged glances, and even the driver threw me a curious bewildered look using his mirror.

I had to get off, at the next stop I lurched off the bus, chest heaving, heart sore from the pain if being surrounded by such sinister people.

I stumbled forward and tripped on the path. People scurried past, eyes to the sky, presumably thinking I was buckled drunk.

Why won't anyone help me? I thought. I struggled back to my feet and tried to walk, then collided with a body. I looked up to apologies and nearly passed out with disappointments. The body was Kevin.

Oh well I decided. Despite the fact that he made my skin crawl, I sobbed into his chest as he held me steady.

My surprise at seeing him left me disarmed, this coupled with having made a whole show of a display of myself, meant that I hastily agreed to his offer of coffee; anything to get off the street. Although I can't pretend that I didn't enjoy how nice he was being to me, fickle I know, but it's not nice to be hated by someone, even an eejit like Kevin.

We slipped into the nearest coffee shop, which wasn't far, for they were all over the city. We found a seat and as soon as I had reduced my stress levels to that of only a mild coronary, he started to talk rapidly.

"Louise, I know you've had a rough time lately, what with everything," he started.

"What do you mean, everything?" I asked, quickly, immediately wary.

"Well, you got mugged last week, remember?" he replied, looking at me like I was mentally subnormal.

"Yes, *I know that,* but how do you?" I replied stoutly.

"I was ehh, talking to your mam," he admitted. "You wouldn't answer my calls, I had to know how you were, I love you babes." He caught my eyes with a smacked puppy dog stare; I resisted the urge to chin him.

"Leave my mother alone you, you fool. I'm fine, I lost my job today, everyone did, our company is closing down, and I'm just stressed is all. It's a lot to happen to a person in a week, I'm feeling a bit down, but I'll be grand," I sniffed. I was defensive, not liking the fact that he had been harassing Mam for information. Not that Mam would have minded, she had always liked him, and also would have enjoyed bemoaning the dangers of cities such as Dublin to him.

"Yeah, yeah, poor Louise," whispered Kevin under his breath, then he realised I had caught him at it, and quickly tried the nice guy/ humble pie approach again.

"I just think, well, let me just take you home and look after you, you need me, Lou, look at the mess you're in, come on, babes, let's go back to mine, and we can cuddle up with a duvet and a good movie," he schmoozed, saying all this as if he was truly expecting me to say yes.

What world did he live in? Was it the same one where I had dumped only weeks ago? Had he no pride?

"Erm, let me just nip to the loo, then we'll order a nice coffee and talk," I smiled tentatively, thinking that this whole thing hadn't been such a hot idea after all.

I ran to the bathrooms thinking, fuck, fuck, fuck. How was I going to get out of this one, I didn't want to hurt him, I also was really in no mood for another coffee shop kick-off / public humiliation today either. I breathed heavily and rested my elbows on the cold bathroom sink. I tried to breathe steadily, but the heat and nerves threatened to overwhelm me again.

"Are you okay, love?" came the voice of an older woman exiting the cubicle behind me.

I saw my reflection and realised that it was a fair question. My puffy, tear streaked face gave me the look of a poorly made up basset hound.

"Not really," I replied with a caustic chuckle. "I lost my job today, had a nervous breakdown on the bus, fell in the street like a wino, then ran into my ex-boyfriend, who's currently waiting out there," I gestured wildly in the general direction of the shop floor, while inhaling rapidly, "trying to badger me into going home with him. Incidentally I'd rather lick the lid of a dog poo bin than do that, just in case you wondered," I finished quietly, diminished by my situation.

"Right," she considered for a moment, "wait here." She marched from the bathrooms briskly.

Where was she gone? To inform the manager and have me thrown out probably, I thought. Or the men in white coats. That was all I needed.

However, she returned and smiled brightly.

"Was he the one with the dodgy hair? He's gone, I told him you had lady's troubles and you'll ring him later." She winked conspiratorially, clearly pleased with herself.

Then she produced a large makeup bag. It was then that I noticed how fabulous she was. Tall, slim, immaculately groomed with cropped blonde hair, like many women her age, but in a cool choppy way. She doused me in potions and lotions then reapplied my makeup – all in a quick, brisk manner, but gently too.

I measured my reflection in the mirror. I looked great to be honest; miles better than this morning anyways. Although this mystery woman had used products that cost more than the average monthly mortgage payment, a far cry from the junk I quickly fire into the trolley at Tesco.

"And for the finale." She elaborately brandished a little brown bottle, like a magician with a rabbit.

"Open your mouth," she told, rather than asked.

I obliged, as if I did so for strangers all the time.

She squeezed three drops of something funny tasting onto my tongue and closed my agape mouth and her forefinger under my chin.

"Rescue remedy," she explained. "It'll calm you right down, I'd give you something stronger, but I keep all the good drugs for myself." She winked again, followed by a dirty laugh.

"As for the job, there's loads of them and it's not worth ruining your makeup over, the man, even less so. Now cheer up, go out tonight with your pals and get scuttered, you'll be a new woman tomorrow," she briefed me wisely, like Dumbledore or Gandalf.

What was this woman? Some kind of angel? I was bowled over by the kindness of this stranger. As if she hadn't done enough, she walked me right to the bus stop and after checking that I had my fare, said goodbye and left. I didn't even know her name. It didn't matter, I knew I'd never meet her again, but I would never forget her. I vowed to repay the favour one day, and show kindness and look after someone in distress. Although I was beginning to think that it might be a while until I was any use to man, beast or anything in between.

Chapter 8

Days passed in a haze of confusion. I was lost, unable to make a productive decision or commit to anything as simple as even a phone call. I roamed the flat, barely functioning as I was so exhausted. The only sleep I did get was unplanned nightmare fuelled broken hours on the couch. I tried to eat, but my mouth was numb, food was devoid of taste, and swallowing was impossible.

It was as if I had been in a car crash, I had survived the impact, but was likely to die of my injuries. I wasn't sad, certainly not happy, I was everything in between. My life was a literal grey area.

My job, my sense of security, my mind – all gone in a week. It's amazing how easy it is to deconstruct a person. At least, it had been easy to deconstruct me.

As if everything else wasn't bad enough, Amanda seemed to be getting fed up of living with a female Eeyore. She tried and tried to snap me out of my waking coma but nothing helped. On Monday, the day I lost my job, Amanda decided that we would get plastered and forget our troubles. I suspected she didn't even want to, which only added to the guilt that already plagued me.

Alcohol didn't help. I was normally a fun drunk. That night I was maudlin, uncommunicative and downright depressing. We gave it up as a lost cause and passed out around midnight. I woke with a hangover like no other. The physical symptoms were bearable, as I felt wretched all the time anyway. The paranoia and shame as becoming such depressive bore was awful though. I spent all of Tuesday in bed, tossing and turning, hunting sleep as a sanctuary from my mind.

On Saturday, Amanda called my parents, even though I begged her not to. I spoke to them for the minimal time I could – long enough for them to sternly tell me that I was to come home for a rest, so they could mind me for a while.

"You're not to be sitting in Dublin all alone, upsetting yourself," said Mam, then she added, in hushed tones, "I know Amanda is doing her best, but she's not the sharpest tool in the box, God forgive me for saying it." I could almost hear her bless herself.

"Yeah, I'll think about it," I said, noncommittally. The thoughts of returning to Lacknamon, or the village of the damned as I usually called it, made my skin flinch. I ended the call, which caused a momentary wave of relief to pass over me. I sighed and rested the mobile against my forehead briefly, nearly being brained as it started to ring again almost immediately.

The screen indicated that Alison was calling. Exasperated, I answered.

"Hello, missus! About time you answered, it's like trying to get Beyoncé on the blower, ringing you!" she gushed, a sharp intake of air told me she was having one of her endless fags.

"I know, I'm sorry, I'm in bed half the time, trying to get any sort of sleep, I'm all over the shop at the minute," I explained, feeling remorseful for not contacting her sooner.

"Don't mind that, I hear you're gone mad, I had your mother on the phone, telling me to check in on you. What's going on, missus?" she asked, gently.

"I don't know, I think its shock after losing my job and getting robbed and all, it's been a bit of a shit couple of weeks," I whined.

I knew Alison, who was a natural fixer, would try to drag me out of my stupor. As I knew I didn't have the motivation to stop her, I tried to pre-empt it.

"I'm not able for any nights out, before you suggest, all I'm good for is my duvet at the minute," I cautioned. Having already ruined Amanda's attempt to party me happy, I didn't want to inflict my company on Alison. I feared I would become that joyless, miserable croon again. The idea of being surrounded by pissed strangers wasn't welcoming either.

Alison's voice jolted me from the scenario playing out in my mind.

"Not at all, not a night out, BUT, I have a voucher for a day of pampering for two at La Vie Da Belle, I got it from Tony for Christmas, and it would only be wasted on him, anyway, he's working in Belfast. So will you come with me? It's supposed to be gorge! We'll get waxed and relaxed and you'll be grand after it." She kept her tone light, but I knew I had no choice. I had to resist regardless.

"I can't, I should be looking for a new job, and well ... to be honest, I don't feel up to it. Besides, why is Tony off again? He's only just back from Sweden." I tried to distract her from what sounded a daunting plan, but I was also curious. Tony worked away a lot, but Alison usually went along. Recently, however, she stayed behind, citing airline costs as horrendous. She was right, of course, unless you want to travel cattle class on some unpronounceable airline, stopping or a night in Azerbaijan, the prices can be arse clenchingly dear.

"Work is work, he has to go, besides, I'll get a bit of peace and quiet, he's learning Spanish to pass the time between jobs, and it's driving me nuts, please, come with me, I don't want to go alone, and the voucher expires soon, you'll love it!" she pleaded.

"Okay," I resigned. I didn't have the energy to fight her, besides; I had one last vestibule of hope. Maybe a day of pampering *would* fix me. I was getting desperate, after two weeks of this hell the temptation to go cap in hand to Dr. Ox was growing with each antsy nightmarish minute.

"Grand, tomorrow morning, I'll get you at ten, seeee ya!" and she was gone. Now that I had committed to something, I was filled with uncertainty. I was afraid, very afraid. The sense of imminent catastrophe was heightened now that I planned to leave my comfort zone. My fear was like a metal gate, shutting off the front door. I itched to call Alison back and cancel. I didn't though, I was too tired and I knew it wouldn't do me any good, I was going, like it or not. The panic was starting to engulf me again and I was shepherded to my room by my sense of dread and an overpowering need to flee. I didn't know what from.

Chapter 9

Sitting in the front seat of Alison's car, with the sun shining, music blaring and us both singing along like teenagers, I tried to embrace the carefree atmosphere and told myself that I had to at least try to escape from this personal Alcatraz I had created.

Today was the day I would feel better, I decided. I'd had enough. Determination and bloody-minded fury fuelled me through the morning routine and into Allison's Mini Cooper. I was gritting my teeth so much that tension fizzled and cracked in jaws. Today is the day, I repeated in my head, like a mantra.

"Any idea what you're going to do about the job situation?" queried Alison.

"Not really, I'm paid until the end of the month and a little bonus so I've time to look for something," I intercepted; before she could start planning job fairs and up skilling.

"Fair enough, but don't get too comfy on your laurels, there's shag all out there anymore, I should know, I've to listen to Tony bitching about it all day, every day. I even had to sack two girls in the bar the last day. They weren't even that shit at their jobs, but I was doing the books and I realised it was a choice between paying them or buying toilet roll for the bar. Although I'm pretty sure they were nicking the toilet roll now, come to think of it," she mused.

"Well, yeah, but I've tonnes of experience –" I started.

"In what's basically a dead market – accounts, admin, even basic secretarial jobs are all being cut down on, trust me, , if you don't want to be a walking sign post down Grafton Street, you need to start looking ASAP. See if that Gobshite Amanda can sort out some dole or something while you wait," she suggested.

I winced at her bitchiness. Despite how much I liked them both, Amanda and Alison had never got on, I had originally thought that it was just a case of clashing personalities, but it turned out that they had a little contretemps in Alison's pub one night. Amanda had been caught serving herself, from her handbag, with a naggin of vodka.

I don't know what Alison's problem was; we had done it enough in our youth. Alison snipped, as though she could read minds. "She's older than you! It's hard enough to turn a profit for my arsehole of a boss without smelly hippies like her sponging off my ambience."

"You shouldn't have barred her though," I protested. "I always feel guilty going without her."

"It's not your fault that she's a cow," answered Alison, in a singsong voice.

"Anyways, enough! We're nearly there, and I've booked you in for a bikini wax along with everything else," she twinkled.

I sighed in resignation. This had long since become a battle of wills, though why the state of my nethers bothered Alison, I'll never know.

Trust Alison to trick me while I was weak, I had resisted for so long! We arrived at La Vie Da Belle and like a lamb to the slaughter; I followed Alison into the glass-fronted, classy-looking establishment. I was glad that it seemed to fall into my favourite genre of spa/beauticians. There was two; the holistic types that were all about plinky plonky watery music and tea tree oil dancing in the air with staff who criticised you for smoking, eating chips and not cleansing, toning and moisturising twelve times a day using paraben-free, alcohol-free, gluten-free gunk that they later tried to sell you at wildly inflated prices.

Then there were the chemically enhanced meccas of beauty that I favoured. They didn't seem to give out as much, but would sort of look at your smoky, greasy, dirty skin and say, "Well, it's not much to work with, but we'll give it a bash, bring out the bleach and my good yard brush!" Then they gently battered you into buying paraben rich, booze-filled gunk at wildly inflated prices.

I'm sorry to say this, I know it's hugely untrendy and unfashionable, but I much prefer the latter. I haven't much time for the hippy dippy approach. My appearance needs lovely noxious chemicals. Grass and oats might be okay for the more fortunate looking few, but it seemed to me that science seemed to have had a good look at what nature had to offer, took all the good stuff, like tobacco, wine and whatever they make eyebrow wax with and then gave a firm "Ah, no thanks pet" to the rest of it.

We approached the bench, otherwise known as the reception desk. Alison, who is never intimidated by beautiful people as she is one, gave a curt, "Booking for two, under Hanlon."

The little blonde receptionist swished her gorgeous blonde head at us, then sighed, pretended she couldn't find our booking, even though I could see it myself on the screen, and told us to take a seat and she would see if there was a free beauty therapist. She supposed. If she must. The gall of us.

We sat tightly on the squeaky faux leather two-seater opposite swishy heads desk for roughly ten minutes. I sat in silence because:

A) I couldn't think of anything to say.

B) Alison was fighting with Tony on the phone.

"Oh, don't be a dickhead, they said it takes ten minutes and we'll know everything the following day ... why? Because it's easier for you that's why! Look, will you just shut up for a minute, we'll talk when I get back," a pause ensued. "I don't know what time, I'm out with Louise, I'll ring you in a bit." She hung up, rolled her eyes, and then scrubbed her face with her hands.

"Right, where's this wan 'till I get my facial?" Alison smiled brightly at me.

"What was all that?" I questioned.

It was unusual for Alison and Tony to fight, let alone for them to resort to name calling, i.e. dickhead.

"Ah, it's a long story," dismissed Alison.

"We have time." I indicated the empty waiting room and pointed out that we had been forgotten about.

Alison nibbled her lip, then sighed.

"I didn't want to say anything ... I shouldn't really. Well, we're trying for a baby, we've been trying for a year, but nothing's happening, obviously. Although if Tony keeps his shitty moods up then I don't know if I want anyone related to him living inside me," she joked, an obvious attempt to dilute the stunned air.

I couldn't believe it. Alison and Tony were the cliché of the "It" couple. He enjoyed weekend breaks, had a stylish house and worked busy jobs. They even occasionally took drugs and drank far past the brink of excess of a weekend. Now they had transformed into potential breeders and all round grownups. My head sizzled, burned and stuck to the grill pan.

"A baby?" I asked incredulously, as if I had never heard such a concept. Then realised I could be misconstrued as being rude.

"I mean, it's great and all, but well, you're not exactly maternal. Remember when you told Oscar that Santa wouldn't come unless he fetched your fags from the other room last Christmas?" Hard to forget, the child was hysterical.

"They say it's different when it's your own, and I am maternal! My mother said the same thing when I told her, but, Louise, I feel so ready for a baby. I'm sick of 3 a.m. tequila shots and dressing up every weekend for gobshites that I don't even like. I'm so bored of being everyone's party girl. It makes me so sad to see other people living normal family lives, when Tony and I still act like students, living off pot noodles and Aftershock. I want a baby and a normal life so bad, and nothing's happening and nobody knows why..." she lamented. I was shocked to see a tear water her eye.

"Fuck, emm, alright, calm down," I soothed, uncertainly.

"What did the doctor say?" Thank god for television, without hospital dramas and soaps, I wouldn't have had a clue what to say to her.

"They want to test Tony's sperm, it's easier to test him first, all he has to do is … you know ... into a cup. You should hear how they want to test me! But, oh my god, you should hear him whinging! That's another thing; the stress of it all is really getting to us. We fight non-stop, especially in the last couple of months with him working away so much. We were so excited in the beginning, now I almost wish we had never even started!" She dissolved into full blown tears and I nearly joined her. I didn't know how she had managed to keep all this to herself.

"Why didn't you say anything?" I asked.

"Because, it's a bit mortifying – being barren. I bet I'm the problem. Tony had a scare with a girl when he was eighteen, but she lost the baby, so it's clearly not him, I've never even had a late period." Alison looked at me, seeking reassurance I think.

To be honest, I was that far gone in my own head, I didn't really have any to give, but I tried.

"I'm sure it's not you. I'm sure there's no problem at all, these things take time," I replied, although I really didn't know. I had spent a great deal of time and money not getting pregnant.

"Well then, when shit-for-head Tony gets back, he's getting tested, and then we'll know," her eyes tightened with determination. Tony didn't stand a chance.

It was then that our beautician arrived. Obviously she was always going to be gorgeous-looking. This one, however, seemed to be determined to make everyone around her spew with self-hatred.

She was all shiny black hair, with a smooth tan and a delicate face that was topped with a pert button nose and a Cupid's bow mouth. Huge brown eyes fell on us with distaste.

Honestly, she looked that appalled at us; you would swear that we had just interrupted a funeral with a farting contest. I was used to the disdain though, I wasn't exactly gorgeous and her sort are always mean little cows.

Alison, on the other hand, quickly regained her adamantium clad brusque persona.

"Is there not supposed to be two of you?" Alison gestured that we were a pair.

"Hi ham Claudette, and zis iz Karmin, we willh be doink hyour treatments today." She ushered a tiny blonde assistant from some unknown corner. Hidden dragon, sleeping manicurist.

This changed everything though! She was French! She was honour bound to be stunning, and sure they hate everyone on account of being jarred on wine and full of goat's cheese and dodgy bread all the time. I warmed to her considerably after this. My boiling envy turned to charm itself and I decided to introduce us.

"Hi ham Lou… erm, I mean, I'm Louise, and this is Alison, erm, thanks," I smiled wanly. Bollocks, my unfortunate habit of imitating people's accents was all well and good when they're on the telly, a totally different kettle o' fish when you're stuck talking to your Scottish granny at a christening.

Claudette yawned deeply, like we were exhausting her and she'd like to lie down on the floor for a sleep. She appeared to change her mind though, and ushered us forward. We followed into a little suite with two bed yokes in it. The room was crammed full of Clinique products, and I wondered if they got them free with Claudette.

"Hi willh start hwith ze hwaxing, then hwe hwill mazzage, after zis, you hare free to enjoy ze sauna, pool and any other facilities," Claudette whispered. "Then before hyou leave, Karmin hwill do Hyour nails for hyou." All of this was barely audible. Claudette sounded *wrecked* and proper fed up with us and our demands. Such a martyr. This was clearly an attempt at being sultry, sexy, and mature a la French woman. However, my mother would be likely to suggest "A good dose of iron tablets and a few ham sandwiches" for that sour puss.

Alison was given a copy of Hello and dodgy cup of something masquerading as tea. She gawked like a drinky teen on gin after the first sip and hastily abandoned it.

Claudette started on my eyebrows which was fine. It was when we worked our way down and she asked me to remove my "Hunderwear" that I started to panic. It wasn't just the pain that frightened me this time. I was feeling quite threatened by exposing my less than toned posterior to her.

I asked her to do my legs first, Alison raised her eyebrows suspiciously.

"Fuck off, I'm working up to it," I told her. I'd do it in my own time, even if I had been press ganged into it. It was a lot like the time she convinced me to have my belly button pierced in Galway. We were both langered drunk, and I woke up the following morning with an ornate chandelier hanging from my midriff.

Claudette baldied my legs, and although I wouldn't describe that as pleasant, it was at least familiar.

"Hokay, now hwe hwill do ze bikini wex!" she intoned. She sounded so solemn that I nearly blessed myself.

I removed "ze Hunderwear" and Claudette slapped on the scalding wax as though she were kneading pizza dough, very palmy.

Then she made it worse by counting down.

"Hwon, two, zree!" She yanked the strip off and actually, looked delighted with herself. An evil smirk crossed her lips. She smiled too early though. The pain hit me and I tried both to swear and to stop myself swearing.

"Fu ... bfff!" I exclaimed.

The result of this was, and I'm puce with embarrassment at the memory, but well, I accidentally spat all over Claudette's head and right arm. The *look* on her face. She was *disgusted.*

I didn't blame her, I was mortified. Alison, on the other hand, was in near convulsions laughing. Tears streamed down her face and she made no effort to stop herself.

"Hexcuse me for a hmoment, pliss," said Claudette, looking rightly fucked off at this stage. She shot a death glare at Alison and briskly exited. She even slammed the door a bit.

Alison wheezed through her laughter.

"Chuffed for her, the unpleasant little wagon," she snorted as she appeared to remember again.

"Stop! Oh my god, I spat on her! I'm humiliated! Will she even come back? We'll be thrown out," I whispered. My face was bright red, I knew it, and I could feel the heat of it.

"Shh, she's coming back," Alison giggled.

Claudette entered and (Spit-free), eyed me like a bull fighter sizing up his bovine opponent in the arena. She side stepped and circled the bed, "Easy now, easy now, girl," then she slapped my rump and threw a red sheet into the air. Well now, she didn't. I'm exaggerating. She did look wary though when she spoke.

"Hwe hwill continue now."

"Ah no, you're grand!" I smiled, whilst pulling on my clothes.

"But iz uneven! Only one part iz done!" Claudette objected.

"It's fine, I don't mind, I like it like this," I smiled, eagerly, searching for mercy, she wasn't having a bar of me though.

"Hno, hno, hno, Iz fine, just leetle more, be fine." She carried on, pulling at my leggings. Claudette clearly wanted revenge. I wasn't doing it again though, no way Jose, or Pierre in her case.

I was already doused in shame after having dribbled on her, now she was trying to yank off my bottoms, hassling me to "Shush now, be fine, no pain."

I wanted to pour the wax into her obviously fake hair and laugh as she nit combed it out. She was practically molesting me.

"Honestly, it's fine, I don't want anymore," I raised my voice in panic, trying to sound firm. I gave Alison a distress signal look.

"I wex quickly, no pain, be fine." She yanked at my trousers again.

"Just Stop!" Alison stood between us suddenly.

Claudette stormed out again. I catch my breath again and, I can't believe it, I'm crying.

The room is too small, too warm, there's no air. I see little black spots in my eyes as I swallow oxygen like a drowning person. Terror rises like a physical wave through my chest as it constricts. Breathing doesn't help, my heart races and my stomach churns. I clasp my hands to my chest and Alison stares, wide-eyed with shock.

Alison tried to settle me on the bed, it's only now that I realise I've been standing. My heart throbs in my ears and the noise is deafening. I hear Alison telling me to try slower breaths, but it's impossible. When I attempt to slow by breathing it comes in loud snivels and yelps involuntarily and that only makes me worse. I have no control over this.

My stomach boils and I feel an almost painful lurch in my throat. Alison hands me a little silver lidded bin and I throw up inside it. The room suddenly spins on its axis. The vomiting did nothing to help me breathe. I cannot feel a single breath enter my lungs, only heat and the tears on my face that obscure my vision. The room rotates again and I feel myself fall to the ground. I'm sure I'm dying. Thank god for that, because whatever is killing me has to be the worst thing that ever happened to anyone.

My head hits the carpeted floor and I feel Alison trying to catch me. Then I know of nothing.

Chapter 10

"Louise? Lou? Can you hear me?" Alison whispered, clearly nervous that I wouldn't wake up, and nervous in case I did.

I was awake, confused, then I remembered that I'd had some kind of heart attack or something. I must be in a hospital I deduced. My head still spun, so I laid still and quiet for a minute or so, then opened my eyes.

I was surprised to find that I was still in the same room at the spa. My breathing was much more relaxed now, though my heart was still racing and I felt dog sick. Shakily, I sat up, with my knees and hands trembling. I wanted to cry again.

I inhaled deeply, and coughed and the acrid taste of vomit. Alison quickly conjured water and I took a huge gulp of it before resurfacing for air, I was starting to realise the joy of breathing and wouldn't ever take it for granted again.

"Louise, did you just have a panic attack?" Alison asked, gently.

Did I? It wasn't the first time that this had happened recently, but I didn't have a name for it so far.

"I don't know, it's happened a couple of times since last week … never this bad though, I've never fainted before," I spoke quietly, ashamed of how pathetic I had become and still stung from the excesses of my panic.

"Since when? Since you got mugged? Your mam said that you'd been a bit off with your sleep and that, but I thought you were just enjoying the time off work, Jesus, Louise, this can't be normal. A cousin of mine went a bit nervy a few years ago, she started losing it like that when she was stressed, but she's fine now, maybe you could see a doctor?" said Alison, stiffly, clearly out of her depth.

I was scared, I was becoming some kind of basket case, and everyone knew, it was clear to see. I was ashamed and I just wanted to escape.

"Can we just go? Please?" I pleaded with Alison.

"Of course we can, do you want to wait here while I get the car?" She stood, rummaging for keys.

"No, let's just leave now, how will we get past Claudette?" I worried, biting my lip.

"Fuck Claudette, she can ask my arse, she was like Gary Glitter with her hands, I wex," Alison imitated her so well that we both snorted.

"Come on," Alison gestured.

"I followed Alison, practically hiding behind her. As we passed swishy heads desk, Alison stopped, swishy head ignored us.

"Listen," Alison tapped the desk. "My friend is unwell, so we'll have to go now, but can you ask the manager to expect my call with a complaint about Edward Scissor hands in there." Alison gestured with her head in Claudette's general direction.

"Sure thing," replied swishy, clearly amused.

We made it to the car, and sped off. I enjoyed the speed, as hasty escape was what I craved. I was so disappointed, I had wanted to enjoy today, and now it was ruined. The guilt of having wrecked Alison's day and most likely her head, was awful too.

"I'm sorry, Al, I don't know what happened, and I know I overreacted. Now your lovely day is all spoiled and they probably won't let you reuse the voucher and you didn't even get anything done for yourself and you're so stressed about real problems and here I am making everything worse over nothing," I gushed, feeling my eyes water again.

"Stop. You're being ridiculous, I don't want a voucher for that kip, I'm sorry I even took you there; you were supposed to feel better. Louise, you're obviously not well, honey, please tell me you'll go to the doctor? I'll go with you if you like? We could go now? Ring up and make an appointment." She passed her phone to me.

I held the phone and hesitated. I couldn't face anymore today. I just wanted to go home, alone. I was exhausted and actually felt that I might sleep. My eyes were heavy and I was finding it hard to concentrate.

"I will tomorrow, I promise, I just want to get home, I've had enough of today," I explained and hoped she would leave it at that. Alison seemed to take my answer and we drove on, I sat in the passenger seat in complete silence and wondered what was happening to me, what had started as shock was now surely taking over my life. I couldn't do anything anymore. Now I wasn't even able to maintain a conversation with Alison, my best friend in the whole world. Alison tried to spark a dialogue, to sooth the uncomfortable silence, pointing out shops and odd-looking people, even bringing up her fertility issues, all I could do was nod and grunt noncommittally. I knew I was being a rubbish friend, but I had no control over it, I could feel this foreign force, pulling me deeper into myself and far away from everything else.

We pulled over, but we hadn't arrived at my place. We had stopped at a corner lined with shops.

"Wait here a minute," Alison peaked quickly. She hopped from the car and I studied her as she entered a pharmacy. She returned ten minutes later, with a bag that rattled. Like a magician, Alison elaborately withdrew two boxes.

"Take two from the blue box at night to help you sleep and three from the green box in the day. They're only over the counter herbal yokes, but they might help until you see the doctor." She smiled and squeezed my hand. I was so touched that I nearly cried (again). I started at my purse to reimburse her, and she waved me off.

"Thanks, Al, I won't forget this, and I really am sorry about today," I said, when we finally arrived at our destination.

"I'll see you during the week maybe?" I hoped she wouldn't avoid me from now on.

"Don't be mad, I'm coming in you dope, I'll put you to bed." She gave me a funny look, almost challenging me to refuse and directed me to my building. I was guided up the stairs, into and through our flat and onto my bed. Alison instructed me into my night things and put on a movie, I don't know what it was called.

I went to brush my teeth, and when I returned I found Alison in my bed, proffering tea. The curtains were drawn, and Alison handed me blue pills and water

"Down the hatch, good woman yourself, I'd take some myself – only I've to drive later," she mused.

I lasted into the opening credits of the movie and then slept while Alison smoked and sipped tea, like a smokey little bodyguard.

Chapter 11

I hadn't intended on breaking my promise to Alison, I really did mean to go to the doctor, but I still hadn't. I was scared that he would tell me that there was no help, that this was just my life now. I knew that people sometimes got medicine, and that they felt better and recovered. I really liked the idea of getting more happy pills that Dr. Ox had given me on that awful day, when it all started.

The other problem was that I rarely left the flat. The only excursions I made were to the dole office and when Amanda would practically drag me by the hand. That was an ordeal in itself, even though Amanda handled my claim and fast tracked everything so that I didn't have to wait the obligatory six months for the pissy little payment.

Today was Valentine's Day, the mugging had happened on the 5th January. The times scale baffled me, because although the days were interminably long, it still felt like only days ago that I first became ill.

I remembered thinking that the "Shock" would pass and being back to normal in no time. I laughed caustically at the thought, I laughed for too long. Amanda looked up from the end of the couch where she was sitting, eyes widened, as though she was scared. I indicated that I was laughing at the TV. Bad idea, the Trocaire ad was on.

I cringed inwardly, and hoped that she would think I was being ironic. Things had been weird between us recently; I sensed that she was growing tired of living with the female equivalent of Jekyll and Hyde. At times, I decided to try to be hopeful, I brushed my hair, cleaned the flat, and even got dressed in an attempt to force myself better by pretending that I already was.

Most of the time, I was overwhelmed by burning, petrifying intrusive thoughts; thoughts that focused on all the wrong things. I spent days wrapped up in my own head, unable to escape it, like a prisoner in my own mind. It was beginning to look like a life sentence, I begged for the chair.

I obsessed over everything. Fancy a cup of tea? But then you'll have to get up, walk to the kitchen and actually make it, are you that bothered, think about it, you're that tired, that you'd probably scald yourself and end up in hospital, sure look at you, they'd never let you out.

Various scenarios played out in my head. Things that happened years ago, being dumped by my first love, failing my French Junior Cert exam, crashing Dad's car into a house on my first driving lesson, all played on my mind; reminding me that I was a huge failure and doomed to misery. These things hadn't particularly bothered me at the time, but it was as though I was feeling all the misery of my lifetime at once.

My concentration was gone; there was just no room for anything good in my mind. I feared that if I stopped anticipating something terrible happening, then it would happen and I wouldn't even be prepared. I felt detached from reality; my actual body felt like a meat suit that hid the real me, which was ensconced beneath layers of pain.

Everything seemed far away, noises were muffled and I couldn't see very far. I remember one morning, lying on my bed and feeling like I was deep at the bottom of the ocean, way beneath where the fish were, alone in deep dark sea.

Alison visited a lot; she still hadn't abandoned me, even when I told her that she should. Her attempts to bring me outdoors were in vain. I never got further than the car without another meltdown. Alison compensated by bringing the world to me, she arrived one Tuesday evening with a new mobile accompanied with strict instructions to ring my parents for their anniversary.

To my eternal shame, I didn't, not because I didn't want to, but I knew that if I spoke to them, I wouldn't be able to keep up a pretence of normality, and they couldn't know how far things had gone, I'd die of shame, and guilt for worrying them.

Today though, I sat on the sofa, like a prize fighter about to enter the ring. I had spent the whole morning psyching myself up. Today: Valentine's Day, was Annie's birthday, and I was determined to call her.

I exhaled deeply, and dialled Annie. She answered on the third ring, right, show time!

"Annie! Happy Birthday!" I actually smiled down the phone, because I knew it would make my voice more convincing.

"Oh, hi, Louise, thanks love, nothing happy about it though. The morning I've had, you wouldn't believe it, your nephew, decided to wake up at god knows what time this morning, and for reasons that elude me, jumped off the bookcase. I've been at the hospital since six this morning, in waiting rooms with mad drunk homeless people and screaming babies and Oscar, who's leg was apparently broken, was running around, bouncing off the walls, not a bother to him. Anyways we're on the way home now, thanks be to Christ, hang on, Louise, Oscar, if you put that tax disc in your mouth one more time, I will redden your arse," Annie snapped.

I couldn't believe it. Obviously, I was very relieved that Oscar was okay, but I was distracted. Annie never shouted at the kids and she certainly never hit them. She had always sworn that she would never, even when Callum was being so bold that Mother Teresa would have gotten an itchy palm.

"What's the matter with you, earth mother?" I asked, almost amused.

"Ah nothin', just a shit birthday so far, it's grand, listen, I have to go, I shouldn't be driving on the phone, the last thing I need today is one of those little fuckin' Hitlers to give me another ticket, I'll call you soon and we'll have a proper chat," said Annie

"Okay, give Oscar a big kiss from me, talk soon, love ya," I piped, with my pseudo elated voice.

I was disappointed; I'd spent ages preparing for that call. It was such a momentous effort to hold my concentration that I'd even written down topics of conversation. I felt short-changed though. Oscar was okay though, the rituals *do* work, I thought smugly.

What it was, was, at odd times I felt compelled to do things. Nothing productive, like look for a job, or make a doctor's appointment, but little inconsequential nonsenses. The first was the tea, if I didn't finish the cup, horror would ensue. Some karmic force was watching, and punishment would be swift. This then extended to eating after 5 o'clock, like some kind of early bird Gremlin. That was an easy one though, I was rarely hungry.

The hard ones were the ones that woke me up. I'd be fast asleep, then I jump awake, have to get up, fight the terror and run up and down the stairs outside our flat ten times, then once more for luck, and once more because I didn't like odd numbers.

I know it sounds insane, but honestly, it helped. After I had done my penance, I could relax almost. I was also fitter and thinner than I had been in years.

Amanda caught my eye and smiled.

"You sound better, that's the most you've spoken all week!" She sounded giddy with excitement.

"Mmmph," I acknowledged.

"Oh," Amanda sighed. "Okay." Her disappointment obvious.

Chapter 12

The weekend had been highly anticipated. I would be alone. Amanda was off to Sligo to visit her parents. "Are you *sure* you'll be okay?" she asked, again and again.

"I'll be fine, I did live alone before you moved in you know," I responded.

I hadn't spent any longer than eight hours on my own in the last month or so, and it wasn't just me who wondered how I would survive.

Alison had offered to come stay for the weekend, but Tony's fertility results would be in on Monday, I would feel too guilty to leave him alone with all that worry on his mind. I made out to everyone that I was looking forward to the alone time, when really I was scared out of my mind. The nights were the worst. To have the security of another person's presence was actually a great help. Not that I woke Amanda up to do the stairs with me or anything, but just knowing she was there helped keep the terror at bay sometimes.

I'd had lots more repeats of the day at La Vie Da Belle. There wasn't even a trigger to it. It could happen at any time. The anticipation of waiting for it was nearly as bad as the attack itself. In fact, I think it brought them on quicker.

Amanda's visit also made me uneasy, she rarely took the mammoth journey to Sligo, and I couldn't help but think that she was only going to get a break from me. I didn't blame her, I'd do the same myself if I could.

Friday afternoon was punctuated with guilty stared on both sides. I felt guilty for exiling Amanda to the wild west and judging from the side long glances and the huge dinner she made, I think she was feeling guilty for leaving, Despite not wanting to be alone, I couldn't wait for her to leave. The tension in the flat was unbearable, when she left, we would both be able to relax.

"I better go, my bus leaves in an hour and there might be traffic, ring me if you need me at all, and I'll come straight back, and Alison said that she would drop by tomorrow as well." Amanda was nibbling her lip anxiously. It was hard to take her seriously, with her beret and pink hair, she looked like and gay allo allo meets lazy town.

I waved her off, "Go, go, go, have a lovely time, bring me back a creepy holy statue," I smiled, in an attempt to dispel the tension.

Apprehensively, she left. I walked her to the door and locked it behind her. Back in the living room I sat, listless, looking around, as if I had never been in it before.

A knock on the door startled me, I realised that Amanda must have forgotten something, that or she was checking that I hadn't put newspaper over the windows and fashioned a lovely tin foil hat to keep the aliens out of my brain.

It wasn't Amanda though, Lovely smiley Mikhal stood at the door.

"I find post for you on the stairs," he twinkled. I looked at the proffered envelope; it was clearly a valentine's card. Probably some marketing shite though, I thought, until I noticed that there was no addresses or stamps on the envelope, it just had my name, Louise, with a couple of kisses beneath it. Whoever it was from had clearly hand delivered it, and my curiosity peaked.

I took the card from him and was about to return to my station in front of the TV, then I remembered my manners, Mikhal was nice, I couldn't treat him like staff as if I was a 20th Century lady of the manner, dismissing him with a flicky wave of my hand.

"Thanks very much, Mikhal, you're very good." I smiled, ignoring the face ache that accompanied it. There, I was off the hook.

"I called him Piotr," Mikhal informed me.

What? I considered. I hoped Mikhal was going to go all old and start reminiscing on me, like Grandpa Simpson. I sighed inwardly and waited for the hour long story about Piotr the grasshopper from when Mikhal was six. A pregnant paused filled the space between us.

"The little cat, I called him Piotr, I keep him." Mikhal smiled enthusiastically, speaking slowly, as if I was simple.

Oooh, the feckin' cat!

"Ah lovely, that's great, a bit of company for you," I said, because that's what you say, isn't it?

"Bye now, and thanks again, ermm, give my regards to Piotr!" I smiled my big smiley head off and closed the door. Great, now I was alienating the neighbours as well, everyone would hate me soon.

I opened the card as soon as the door closed. I was *dying* to know who had sent it.

A small yellow bird paraded on the front, a bunch of posies in his beak. Quite an ambiguous card for Valentine's Day. I wondered if this was from Mrs Upstairs, disguising hate mail.

I opened it and read:

Louise,

Thinking of you, Ring me! !
Happy Valentine's day

Kevin
Xxx

Ah Shite. I wished he would just piss off. There's at least a million people in Dublin, could he not go and annoy the arse off some other girl? If it wasn't cards, then it was flowers and texts and missed calls at 4 a.m., when he was presumably plastered. I gave the flowers to Amanda for her mammy and had started to turn my mobile off at night,

I flung it onto the hall table and went back to watch telly. Checking the sky menu, I realised that I had missed the first ten minutes of *Gavin and Stacey* because of him and his card. Resentfully, I retrieved the card and drew a willy and a beard onto the bird. A speech bubble above it now read "Kevin is a knob head." That was better.

Childish I know. Feck it.

Chapter 13

Friday night remained uneventful, and even though the sickly heat, cotton wool brain and general crap feeling hadn't yet passed, I had at least not suffered a mini breakdown in ooohh, at least a day, which in my mind signified progress.

Saturday morning, I even managed breakfast, something which rarely happened these days. I was never hungry, but in the mornings I usually felt so sick from lack of sleep and mental exhaustion that the idea of eating seemed insurmountable. Food, which I used to enjoy (a bit too much) tasted plain and unappealing. I had tried everything to encourage my appetite, but along with everything else in my life, eating had lost its lustre.

I knew I had lost weight, a good bit actually. While previously, this would have had me ecstatic and out in the shops buying miniscule jeans that I would never actually wear, I now barely noticed. My concave hips and flat stomach waved up at me "here, look it's us! Haven't seen you in a while eh, fatty?" I couldn't bring myself to care though.

After breakfast I attempted to watch television again. I was so frequently in front of that little black box, that I found myself looking away from it, to check a text or whatever only to discover that several hours had passed.

I didn't even focus on what I was watching, programme after programme washed over me, by the end of one episode of *EastEnders* I would still be none the wiser as to who was having an affair or whatever. I still couldn't bear to have it turned off though; silence left my mind to wander. My idle mind was like an unguarded gatepost, and feelings of paranoia and imminent catastrophe flooded in if left unchecked.

That morning, however, I had an irresistible urge to put my foot through the screen. I was sick to death of it. I switched channels to loose women. High pitched nasal voices screeching about feminism and enforced male slavery pierced my brain and I decided the TV would be safer turned off.

"What now?" I spoke aloud, and then felt silly. I found that I had been tapping my fingers against the arm of the couch without realising that was always happening. I had developed lots of quirks and subconscious habits, my nails were fecked beyond belief. I noticed a red wine stain on the couch, I really must do something about that, I thought. I had postponed the cleaning on the night of the Christmas party on account of being langered.

I remembered that night fondly. Amanda and I had spent days readying the flat. We hid anything breakable or expensive (one lamp that had been a gift from my mother) and rammed our fridge full of drink.

You know the sort, these were the people who insisted that they could only have one or two, crying work/nieces christening/triple bypass in the morning. Such composure never lasted long and they were usually found sneaking out of your spare bedroom the following morning. Pasty green while the horrific object of their booze fuelled affections slept on.

It was the Christmas party that I had first tried to finish with Kevin. I may have overdone it on the sauce (tequila) and was dancing on the coffee table with Amanda when I ended our love affair. I don't actually recall it very well to be honest, but Amanda informs that that I called him a big girly gobshite and gently implied that he had lesbian's hair.

I woke up the following day, dying a thousand deaths, but otherwise delighted to be shot of him. Kevin, of course, decided that it had been the booze talking. "That's just what we do, babe, we fight, but we make up, we're passionate!" he enthused. Did he think we were Blake and Amy or something?

I then sat him down, on neutral territory (coffee shop) and explained that while I was grateful for his hard work, I would have to let him go, collect your p45 on the way out and don't expect a reference if you get me.

Anyways, I decided that now would be a good time to get rid of the wine stain. I loved our couch, lime green and stuffed to bursting point. Very funky I decided when I first moved in, then set about redecorating the entire room like a seventies nightclub.

The lava lamps and beaded doorways didn't last long. Amanda described it as "Like being at a hippy love-in" when she first saw it, and I will admit that I may have gone overboard. I scrubbed and scrubbed with a bristly yoke and a basin of chemicals, but the stain didn't budge, I had heard that white wine was good for removing its red counterpart, but if I had the energy or inclination to visit the off license, I certainly wouldn't waste it on the couch. The doorbell rang and I ran to answer, hoping it would be Alison. As an alcohol veteran from years behind the bar, I thought she might know how to shift the stain.

"Howaya!" I chirped into the intercom.

"Garda Connor Grady here for Louise Casey," came a thick, west of Ireland, accent.

I buzzed him through. Hope sprung in me. Maybe they had found muggerman. Since going a bit mad, I had, in desperation, started to scour the internet for magic cures and came across many theories. Months ago I would have laughed at the American cliché of "Closure" but lately I had been thinking that maybe if "Muggerman" was caught, I would be able to move on. Like I say, I was desperate.

Garda Connor Grady didn't exactly incite any great confidence in the might of the blue fury for me. Despite being about forty feet tall, he looked about nine stone, soaking wet. His childish face was framed by and undefined hairless jaw, thick glasses and sandy blonde hair. He looked about ten.

After I beckoned him inside, he stood awkwardly in the sitting room, shifting his weight between his feet and pulling his fingers.

"Sit down," I invited.

"Emmm, yeah, grand," he obliged, flipping a note pad open. "Now, I'm here to follow up on our enquiries following the alleged incident in January. Do you have any further information for us? Anything you remember?" He asked this with his little black notebook and pen in his hand, poised for action.

I was outraged! *Alleged incident?!* Well over a month had passed and they wanted to know if I had remembered anything new? Was this as far as they had gotten?

I had entertained notions of CSI type investigations: men in white lab suits performing really intelligent forensics in that laneway. Did they not even have a CCTV?

Suddenly I was more than outraged, I was *furious!* I was sick of being a victim, sick of being so frightened all the time. My whole life had been ruined by this one event and the useless bastards that were supposed to help were probably sitting in a layby, harassing people speeding to the school gates and eating snack boxes.

I yelled my frustrations at the him, although I was in such a blind fury that I can't really remember what I said. I caught the end of my last sentence though. "…off your fat useless arses and catch the bastard!" I was yelling fit to burst. I only wished Mrs Upstairs would come down to complain, I was well able for her today.

To my disbelief I found his eyes were watering, his bottom lip quivering a long pause ensued while we both waited to see if he would break. He did. It was awful.

"I wish, heeh, people would, huh huh, stop shouting at me!" he cried, between snotty breaths.

"Ah here, it's alright, I'm sorry, I didn't mean it, you're grand really," I tried to console him, his tears made me uncomfortable, although I was in no position to judge.

"I didn't ask for this, it's not fair! It's not my fault we haven't caught the fella who mugged you. I thought it would be different, like in *24*! But it's not, people just shout at me all the time." He stared at me with red tea-filled eyes, as if beseeching me to understand.

I fought down the urge to laugh, and made him a cup of tea. Then he proceeded to tell me all his problems. It seemed that he only became a policeman because his mother thought it would be good, and out of a lack of any better ideas.

Coming from rural Galway he had no idea what was waiting from him in Store Street Station, in the heart of Dublin.

"I can't do anything right so the Sargent was shouting at me this morning. I was supposed to be here, getting info on this case, and now I've made a right balls of that, too!" he started to sob again.

The poor lamb, I too had known the loneliness of a strange city, a tough new job and the homesickness that accompanied it.

"How long have you been in Dublin?" I gently asked.

"Two weeks!" he sniffed, big round blue eyes staring back at me.

I sighed.

Chapter 14

After he left, I felt, to put it bluntly, browned off. I could barely handle my own misery, let alone his. I also had a fierce sense of injustice on his behalf. He reminded me of a little lost orphan, like Harry Potter or Oliver twist ... or an X factor contestant.

I felt terribly guilty for shouting at him, too. Even if the memory of this hugely tall policeman crying on my couch did make me want to giggle a bit. He left after an hour, but before I released him, I made him wash his poor red little face and applied Beauty flash balm to it as he looked like he had been bawling. I had a feeling this wouldn't go down well with the lads at the station. It didn't do much good though, he started to cry again because someone was finally being nice to him.

I waved him off and he looked a great deal more chipper than earlier. I gave him my new number, and he gave me his. Not in a sexual way, of course, but because I had promised to take him on a night out and show him the ropes when I was a bit better, but only if he was good.

I gave up on the couch stain, the only plus side being that Connor had been sitting on it, so it was now mostly dry.

After all the scrubbing and Dr. Phil impressions, it was going on four in the evening. I was, as usual, exhausted, and decided to have something to eat and go to bed. I had enough of the daytime.

I toyed with the idea of ringing for a Chinese. I was still lacking in motivation and energy, and if the food tasted nice, then I might actually eat it. Then I remembered my dwindling finances and abruptly changed my mind.

Beans and toast I decided, grand! And maybe a couple of the lovely blue pills. I could feel the overwhelming misery ebbing in and I decided it pre-empt it. Fearing the fear, if you will.

The stuff Alison bought me from the chemist didn't really help. They weren't a patch on the lovely sedatives from the Doctor, but I used them because they at least made me feel like I was doing something. A placebo effect, I thought, then stopped myself, if it was a placebo effect, then I didn't want to know.

I swallowed two of them, then two more for good measure. I breezed through the kitchen, turning things on and setting up the toaster.

Humming and flapping around, full of nervous tension. I began to feel breathless. Quickly, I lit the gas ring and slapped a pot of beans onto it. I yawned deeply and decided to switch on the TV while everything heated up. First, I sat upright on the couch, then my shoulders, my shoulders felt tight, so I relaxed them and slumped a bit. Still, I wasn't comfy, and then I put my feet up and found the imprint of my form. I think it had been indented from all the hours I had sat, prone in this very position.

I yawned again and relaxed my muscles. This made a pleasant change; I even unfurled my face from its usual frown. My eyes watered, I closed them. This was the best I had felt in so long. The sun came through the window and I felt it's warmth on my face. A gentle breeze danced through the room and I inhaled it slowly. The air felt clean and calming.

I'd stay here for five minutes I told myself. Then I promptly fell asleep. As I sunk beneath the layers of consciousness I wondered, how was this so easy? Was *it* the herbal pills? They had never had this effect before, then again, I'd never taken four at once before. I hadn't felt this chilled in ages, but I couldn't get rid of the feeling that I was forgetting something.

Chapter 15

The smoke alarm in the kitchen didn't work. It didn't work because Amanda had once belted it off the ceiling with a sweeping brush after cremating a pizza.

So the first indication that something was amiss, was, the smoke alarm in the hallway screeching. I jolted awake to find that I had been drooling in my sleep.

My eyes were stinging, thick black smoke plumed from the kitchen, through the small hallway, and seeped into the living room.

Standing up, I couldn't see a thing, the smoke was too thick. It was like breathing dust, my chest wheezed and ached as I crawled towards the kitchen. When I reached it I saw the flames, coughing and blind, I tried to find out where the source was. Orange and blue fire licked the curtains. I tried to bat them out using my hands, burning my fingers.

The heat forced me backwards. I ran back to the hallway. Even though I had never been a MENSA candidate, my common sense abandoned me. I fell to the ground, breathing heavily, grateful for the slightly cleaner air. The smoke bellowed out from the kitchen in an almost solid-looking wall. I was edged further away, until I was back into a corner beside the front door.

My eyes and ears burned from the smoke and noise of the alarm, which was deafening. I covered my ears with my hands and closed my eyes, to drown out the sensory overload.

I'm going to die, I thought, regret and sadness overcame me and I sobbed, I thought of my parents, they would be devastated and so annoyed by my pointless death. I imagined my family, be-suited at a graveside. Hysterical now, I sobbed on. Amanda and Alison swam into my mind, Amanda would have to move, her home burnt to the ground. Alison would probably be better off, they all would really.

Time passed as I crouched in the corner. I knew I should be doing something, but I was literally frozen with fear. Even with my eyes and ears blocked, I could still smell the smoke and flames. My chest tightened and I coughed until my throat felt like it too was alight with embers.

A cold whoosh of air it my left side and I nearly passed out with relief. Oxygen! Clean, cool, breathable air! I noticed the door was open and saw the back of someone run towards the kitchen.

"Louise?! Louise?! Where the fuck are you?" Alison's hysterical voice came from the kitchen; I heard her cough and splutter. I tried to call back, but I was too choked.

Mikhal shortly followed her, but unlike Alison, he noticed me behind the door.

"I have her! Come on, out! She's fine," he called to Alison.

I felt myself being hoisted and carried away.

At this stage, I was so dazed, drunk on oxygen and spent from crying, I didn't realise until I felt the pressure of a couch under me that I was in Mikhal's apartment.

Mikhal disappeared, brandishing a huge red fire extinguisher. I lay in the strange new environment savouring the fresh unsullied air. I could still smell the vicious smoke, on my clothes, up my nose and across the hall.

I scanned the room between coughing fits and breathing. It was astonishingly well ordered and neat. A little lamp table huddled next to an armchair beneath the window. Spotless pale blue walls and rows and rows of books on shelves lined the room, all arranged by size. The carpet underfoot was soft and spotless, like new, only nicer. It was clearly a room inhabited by one. I began to feel sorry for Mikhal, I hoped he wasn't lonely.

I didn't get much time to worry about Mikhal's social life though. Alison and Mikhal entered the room, slightly breathless but otherwise fine.

"Are you okay? Are you burnt? Oh look at your poor hands!" Alison rushed to my side and inspected the damage.

"I'm grand, it's only a small burn, is the fire out?" I asked. I couldn't hear the smoke alarm anymore; I hoped this was a good sign.

"Yeah, it was just the curtains and a few wires, why was the cord off the toaster on the hob?" she asked, severely.

"I don't know, honestly! I was making dinner, but I fell asleep, and ... I'm sorry, I'm so sorry." I began to cry, panic rendering me useless once more. This was excruciatingly embarrassing. I had nearly burned the house down, and was now crying all over my rescuers, one of whom, I barely knew. It was actually the second time he had been forced to save me, that made it worse.

Speaking of Mikhal, he was standing awkwardly behind Alison. He seemed to start off saying something, and then changed his mind. He shuffled from the room, muttering about something to drink.

"Louise, tell me the truth ... did you start the fire ... on purpose?" asked Alison, gripping my hand, clearly desperate for the right answer.

"No! Of course not! I'm just a fucking liability who apparently can't even cook beans on toast without causing a fire, it was an accident, I promise," I said, staring into her eyes, pushing her to believe me.

"Okay, right, well, you're coming home with me tonight –" she started.

"I can't, the flat, it's probably a shambles! I'll be fine," I shook my head, discounting the idea.

"The flat will be fine until tomorrow, you're coming home with me, I'm calling the doctor and we're going to sort this out!" she commanded, giving me a look that spoke "None of yer guff!"

I didn't have the strength to fight her. I could feel my mind collapsing in on itself already. The sooner I did what she wanted, the sooner I could take to me bed. Any bed. I found this happening a lot recently. I threw myself into things to get them over with, not enjoying them, just appeasing everyone else. If it was left to me, I'd do nothing, but I did them, so that I could be left in solitude to get on with the business of my own lonely lunacy.

Mikhal returned, "Here, is good for shock, is Polish drink." He gave us one of his twinkly eyed smiles, and I honestly felt better.

I swallowed the strong smelling liquid, and surprisingly didn't puke.

"Right," said Alison, finishing her drink in one gulp. "I'll ring a taxi, you go grab some bits from your flat," she ordered.

"Thanks so much, Mikhal, for your help and the key and everything, you're a lifesaver, literally!" she thrilled.

"What key?" I demanded. I was currently very big on security.

"Amanda, she leave me key, in case there is an emergency, then I hear your friend knocking and the alarm, so we used it, I hope you don't mind." Mikhal looked concerned.

"No, no, of course not." God, the rudeness of me, the man had run into a burning flat for me. Even so, I didn't appreciate Amanda getting a babysitter. It was embarrassing, although the fact that I was a looper was fast becoming public knowledge.

"C'mon you, we'll get out of this man's hair," scolded Alison. I resented her condescending tone, like I was a bold child causing trouble. Then I remembered everything she had just done for me and copped onto myself, feeling ashamed.

Chapter 16

The kitchen was a state. The worst was surrounding the cooker. Plastic was melted onto it, and now I could see the remnants of an electrical cord charred over it. I followed the cord to the toaster, which although black on one end seemed fine. There was even two pieces of perfect toast poking comically out from it, mocking me.

The curtains hung in tattered soggy strips. I presumed that was the fire extinguisher, everything was soaked. The smoke damaged wall had foamy drips sliding down it, leaving grubby stripes in the paint.

I sighed, this was all I needed. Not only the expense of fixing, replacing and cleaning everything, but the same of telling Amanda that I had nearly burnt her every possession to pieces, because *I fell asleep.*

Alison shooed me to my room and I noticed that, despite the smokey smell, the rest of the apartment was fine, the windows were open and the air was beginning to clear as well. This cheered me, for about a second. I half-heartedly threw a toothbrush, clean clothes and pants into a bag.

We turned the electrics off "Just in case" assured Alison and left. I felt like I was leaving both a warzone and my only safe haven.

Alison, god love her, fielded all the idle chit-chat with the taxi driver. "Where are you going?"

"Have you been on long?"

"Is town busy?" The usual guff that people used in taxis, or indeed, when they paid anyone for a direct service. It stems from the over polite, guilt complex that every Irish child is given at their holy communion. The urge to ensure someone that yes, I am paying you to do this, but, *I'm not posh, I'm just like you!* Which is of course true, but everyone feels a bit grandiose when people are doing stuff for them. You couldn't be seen to enjoy it though.

When we arrived at Alison's, we had a small scuffle over who would pay. Alison fuelled by her instinct to mind me and me trying to replay her interminable kindness.

I won in the end, by thrusting twenty quid at the driver, insisting that he keep the change, (who did I think I was, Daddy Warbucks?). He did deserve it though, the pungent smell of smoke off us was pretty ... distracting, let's say.

Alison lived in a smart two bed townhouse in Dun Laoghire, because she was an actual adult, unlike me, she owned her house. The day she signed the dotted line and took ownership was one of great rejoicing. Alison displayed the deeds proudly amongst her friends. Then promptly lost them somewhere in one of the endless nightclubs in Temple Bar. To this day she hasn't found them, and Tony still doesn't know.

I would love to be given a blank cheque book and free reign in Alison's house. Not that it wasn't nice, it was. It was just a bit minimalist, like a doctor's surgery. All the walls were brilliant white, the furniture was made of glass and chrome, even the couch, ah no, I'm only joking, but it was white leather. There was no colour, I liked colour. In fact, and don't tell her I said this, I sometimes describe Alison's house as anaemic.

After mentally redecorating the entire living room, I flopped on the couch, which felt like a park bench. Alison went to find Tony; I presume she was successful in her mission, shortly after I heard whispered words.

"Of all the days, Alison," whined Tony.

"I could hardly leave her there, Tony, she needs me, I'm her best friend," said Alison, anger catching her voice.

"I know, I know, it's just, their calling in the morning, I would have liked to have been able to ... discuss things," Tony muttered.

Then their voices quietened to a level that only dogs could hear, so I gave up trying to listen.

Alison walked into the room and presented me with towels.

"Shower for both of us, we smell like a teenagers bonfire." Alison sniffed her jumper, and then recoiled, nose wrinkled.

The bathroom didn't mismatch the rest of the house, white and chrome, everywhere. Even though I could feel the heating on, it was cold. It felt like it might cut you to look at it, it was that sharp.

I quickly scrubbed off in the shower, in and out very quickly. On the plus side, Alison had all manner of lovely scrubs and soaps. Not that I was much interested. Personal Hygiene wasn't high on my list of priorities. To be honest, I hadn't managed more than a once over with a baby wipe recently.

Even though it was only seven in the evening, I wore pyjamas. I needed comfort to hide in and my dressing gown; a big pink fluffy affair enveloped me. I snuggled into its warmth.

I waited for Alison, who was in her en suite, on her bed. My hair was dripping everywhere, but I didn't know where the hair dryer lived, and I was scared to look for it. I always suspected Alison of having a dark side, and I didn't want to find evidence of some sordid sex life.

When Alison finally returned, looking fragrant, she studied me, and then sat.

Again, she took my hand.

"Louise, why didn't you do anything to stop the fire?" she asked.

"I couldn't, I was literally not able do anything to help myself. I'm so embarrassed. I'm not the person I used to be, Al, what's happening to me? Why am I suddenly like this?" I implored her for an answer.

"I'm not sure, I think it's something to do with the mugging though, you might have post-traumatic stress thingy maybe? Either way, I want you to listen to me, don't freak out, just listen; maybe you should go to your parents for a while –?"

"What? I will not, I'm bad enough as it is, without going to the village of the damned!" I laughed it off.

"Louise, you need to be looked after, and I can't do it right now, what with work and ... everything else, so staying with your parents would be the best thing for you right now. I promise, you'll feel like a new woman when you get there. Let your mammy spoil you for a few weeks, see a doctor, just relax for a bit, it's like a holiday! When you get back I'll take you on the biggest night out you've ever been on." Alison smiled encouragingly, as though she could will me to agree.

"Alison, why are you saying all this like it's already been agreed? You haven't ... you didn't ring them?" I asked, horrified.

In all fairness, she did have the good grace to look ashamed.

Chapter 17

Alison thought it would be best for me to go back to Lacknamon. Easy for her to say.

I didn't relish the idea of going home. I felt like my world had become much bigger than had been when I left, nearly 10 years ago. I remembered one summer from when I was about fifteen. The circus had, for reasons only known to themselves, decided to come to Lacknamon. There was great excitement amongst the local youth, who I suppose were getting bored of harassing the protestant English children that had moved to the town only six months earlier.

The poor circus performers had barely time to unpack their leotards and oversized shoes when the community council (like the mafia but with more tweed and more powerful) descended. The head hauncho, Anne Maguire, sternly marched up to a man carrying loads of tarpaulin around the supersavers car park. To this day nobody knows what she said to him, or why he didn't just tell her to fuck off for herself, but the circus packed up and left that day, and funnily enough, so did the protestants.

I could imagine it now, the nosy neighbours, feigning familiarity, just to find out if you were late paying your electric bill ... god, it would be awful.

I did, however, feel drawn to the idea of going home. To have my mam mind me until I was well enough to resume normal service. I could almost smell the home cooked dinners, and the lovely crisp bed sheets that always smelt of lavender. Unlike the sheets I washed, which seemed to always smell of socks, no matter what I did. I'd be able to sleep for days, knowing that my family stood between me and the rest of the world.

As vain as it sounds, I knew my parents would be delighted to have to look after me. Recent phone calls had indicated that my parents were suffering from some form of empty nest syndrome. Either that or the telly was broken, because they had taken to calling me at eight in the evening, *EastEnders* time.

Suddenly the idea of cuddling into a big warm parental blanket started to appeal to me.

Chapter 18

I was (once again) terrified. This time, however, I had good reason, Dad, who didn't have a lot of experience of driving in Dublin city, had collected me from Alison's early that morning.

After trying for an hour to direct him to my house, so I could collect my things for my exile, we have ended up on the motorway to Donegal, completely the wrong direction. After somehow managing to get in the direction of Cork, where Lacknamon was, Dad didn't want to risk the big city again.

"Dad, we've got to go back, I've no clothes!" I explained, gently, he was looking a bit pale since that man had flicked him the Vs. Talk about an overreaction, did he think he *owned* the bus lane?

"You can buy new clothes," Dad replied.

"I've no money," I counteracted.

"I'll give you money," Dad offered.

Grand, I thought, that would do nicely. Then I remembered, my laptop – my link to normality! We'd have to turn back I informed Dad and he paled even more.

"We can buy another one of them too!" he offered, anxiously. The look on his face said "Please, please, don't send me back there," as though he had just escaped 'naam. I took in his worried eyes, and then remembered reversing down a pedestrianised street only twenty minutes previously.

"Okay, forget it," I sighed.

Dad accelerated and pelted out of the city before I could change my mind. We trundled along the motorway for a good forty minutes until we approached the toll bridge.

Dad had a small coronary when he realised how much he was expected to pay. I couldn't help but agree, but it couldn't be helped, it had to be paid, otherwise the toll bridge troll who worked in the department of transport would get you in the night.

Dad threw change at the little catch basket yoke on the unmanned booth. He threw it quite hard though, and most of the change bounced back, hit Dad and rolled under the car.

I could hear Dad under his breath, "For *fucks sake!*"

He got out to retrieve the change, and then returned looking sheepish.

"I ehh, can't fit under the car, you'll have to go." His eyes skitted to the three cars behind us, beeping.

I had no choice, we had no change. So, in the only set of clothes I had, I belly crawled under my dad's Polo, trying not to think about the chewing gum and fag butts beneath me.

I wasn't even allowed to just grab the change and go. Dad insisted that I stay under the car until he had counted the change, to ensure it was all there. On and on he counted, slowly, like a half blind geriatric in the Tesco queue.

Once the final count was established, and the change deposited in the *stupid fucking basket,* Dad hurried me into the car, and took off at speed, convinced that the barrier was on a timer and would crash down any minute.

We finally set off again.

I tried to sleep, but the neck rest was uncomfortable, I laid my head against the window and it rattled noisily, shaking my brain. I sat up and Dad started on what I knew would be a two hour tirade of small talk. Strangely enough, I fell asleep quite shortly. I slept all the way to Lacknamon. We eased up the driveway and I caught a glimpse of home. Our primrose yellow bungalow, with the porch I sat in on many a rainy day. I was glad to be home, for about a minute. We approached the front door, when it suddenly swung open, revealing a tiny little woman, with a typical Irish Mammy hairdo: short and curled in on itself from a night in heated rollers. To look at her, you would think she was quiet, soft-spoken, *normal* at least. More fool you.

Like a soprano, she bellowed, "Jesus, Mary, and Joseph, the cut of you, thin as a whippet! Get in, it's freezing, the dinners on, we'll have a cup of tea and you can sit down, I'd say the journey took it out of you. Though some people say that car journeys are relaxing, I don't get it myself though, I do get out with whiplash after driving with your father, *very* tough on those breaks, he is…" Mam waffled on, rotating me like a chicken on a spit roast, then caught herself, seeing my harassed expression.

"How are you, pet? Don't worry, you're home now, we'll mind you," she softly crooned, hugging me. Her eyes met mine and held my gaze, I felt myself unburdening myself, like a buckaroo donkey.

Here you go, Mam, here's my problems, take them, fix them and give them back washed, dried and ironed – I thought.

Dad had busied himself getting my "Luggage" (one bag) from the car, and then we all went inside.

Chapter 19

On my first night home, after being force fed herculean amounts of food as Mam watched closely, I started to wonder whether I had done the right thing. After only an hour I felt myself becoming smothered. I wanted to run to my room and lock the door, turn on my angsty teenage music and block out the world.

After dinner, it started, I knew it would, it would be terrible, but like everything else recently, I would get it over with.

"Louise, what's going on, pet?" asked Mam, Dad nodded and looked at me expectantly.

I had known this was coming. My parents, who liked to fix everything, would want to know where to start. I knew my sanctuary would be given regardless of whether I answered them or not. I decided, however, they deserved an explanation as to why their twenty-six-year-old daughter had arrived home, at a time when they should be going on cruises and being ripped off by Spanish villa developers, like normal retirees.

I voiced this to them, and they looked confused, weirded out in fact.

I carried on regardless. Not that I was planning on telling them the whole story. For example, I would not be telling them that I sometimes felt like I was under the ocean, or that I had all the sadness of the world swilling in my mind and I constantly wished I could remove my head, and just cease to exist for a while, or forever. I also didn't tell them that I was pretty sure I was here to stay. I knew only a couple of things for definite, I was no longer equipped to deal with my current life, it was hard, unsuccessful, and downright depressing. I decided to give up on it. I was going to hide in the bosom of my family. It seemed safest, especially now that I had given up on getting better. I knew this because I wasn't really ill; I was finally just seeing the world for what it was.

So I would allow my parents to try to "fix me", to piece back the person that I once was, and when everyone realised that I was a lost cause, I could spend my days in my parents' house. Spinster of the parish. People would walk past my parents' house, and whisper, "That's where that Casey child lives, a lovely girl, but a bit gone in the head." I would wear tweed suits and middle part my hair, which would have long grey roots. I might even have bottle end glasses, even though I didn't wear glasses.

It didn't sound like much of a life, but it sounded safe and that's what I needed. So when I turned to my mother, to answer her question as honestly as I could, I breathed deeply.

"I'm not sure what's going on. I've been a bit down recently, but I think I'll be okay after little holiday, it just might … take a while," I hinted, widening my watery eyes for effect.

"I'm not sleeping very well, or eating or … anything really, I think I've a small touch of depression or something," I intoned, to the floor, ashamed to meet their gaze.

"We'll go see Dr. Harper in the morning so, love, and you get a good sleep tonight, you'll be a new woman," decided Mam, with her business head on.

"Who? Where's Dr. Coyne?" Dr Coyne was the doddery old doctor that my parents went to. I had looked forward to seeing him, as he would readily provide the pills. He wasn't so much, into regulations as other doctors might be.

"Dr. Coyne retired two years ago, Dr. Harper is our GP now, lovely woman, she takes a holistic approach to health, myself and Margaret Maguire go to her spiritual healing classes on a Wednesday, and your father is helping young Pearse Harper with his cyber café, where we did the computer classes, no head for accounts the poor love, but the things he can do with a computer!" Mam rattled.

A cyber cafe? In Lacknamon? She might as well have told me that they were having a gay pride march in every Thursday on the main street.

I expressed my shock to Dad by telling him this.

"Ah no," he guffawed. "Sure the LGBT March was last July, Bill Deasy and his pals organised that from the school. Your mother made sandwiches in O' Connors afterwards," said Dad, matter of factly.

What? Was I hallucinating? Had I really lost it now?

Last time I checked, it was still practically illegal to be gay in rural Ireland and they still thought that Satan ran the BBC.

It was then that I noticed the top of the range PC at the back of the kitchen.

"When did you get that?" I asked Mam.

"Oh that yoke." She eyed it suspiciously.

Good woman, I thought, don't have anything to do with the devil box.

"That's your fathers, I don't like it all, it runs Windows 7, and I prefer the Mac so I just use the iPad," she explained, pragmatically.

I nearly fell off the chair.

"I'm going to bed," I told them, and that's what I did.

Chapter 20

I woke up the following morning, sweating and tangled in the sheets. Where was I? Then I remembered yesterday. Oh Jesus … I moaned. I was visiting the hippy dippy GP today for my "Magic Cure."

I also had the overwhelming feeling that I had forgotten something of upmost importance … what was it? I had forgotten to … worry! I slept all night, ate well after 5 p.m. and didn't give my fears *nearly* enough attention. I nearly puked with fright, what could have happened? Anything. I tentatively got up.

I wandered through the house; all seemed fine, the apocalyptic consequences of my incompetence didn't seem to have happened yet, at least not in the immediate area. I began to fret, my mind in overdrive. Where were Mam and Dad? Their room was empty, as was the rest of the house. I checked the drive, like a mad woman in the garden in her pyjamas. There was no car there. I ran back into the house, I'd call Mam I thought. I ran too quickly for that time of the morning and skidded on my elbows on the gravel. I got straight back up, no time to assess the damage. I went towards the phone, only to hear the sound of gravel cracking in the drive.

"Mam? Where were you? I was so worried, is everyone okay? Annie? The kids? ... Dad? Brian?

"What? Their grand, I was just dropping off flowers at the multi-denominational church, Simone Guptra is in getting her veins done so I'm standing in." Mam looked shocked to see her adult daughter, snivelling and scabby kneed, like a three-year-old.

"I'm sorry, Mam," I whimpered, sinking to the ground. My stomach started to heave again, with relief or shame or god knows what. I retched and retched, in the garden, in my pyjamas.

After I stopped, my body sagged, and I breathed slowly for nearly ten minutes. I (again) started to cry. I cried like my heart was breaking, because it was. Not just my heart either, I was broken. I couldn't take the strain of being me anymore. It was too hard. I kept my eyes closed, because I couldn't bear to look at Mam. I had seen her face when she first came home, confused and frightened. I had done that to her, my lovely mam. The shame was palpable. I was the most selfish human on earth. Why couldn't I have just stayed in Dublin? How could I have thought I could just offload all this … *shit* on my parents. I felt my head being lifted and then rested on Mam's lap.

"Shhh," she whispered.

We stayed that way for ages. I didn't look at Mam, I couldn't, but I had a horrible feeling that she was crying, too. When I finally regained the strength needed to walk and exist again, Mam half carried me into the house.

Chapter 21

In … out … in … out … hmm, I wonder how old I was when I put that Britney poster on the ceiling … State of her hair, I'd be mortified, I sometimes feel sorry for celebrities, having all that photographic evidence of their fashion faux pas ...

Shit … I've wrecked it. I was supposed to be practicing my breathing/relaxation techniques. The girl at the mental health centre had taught me all these methods for preventing my "little attacks". It was nearly a month since Mam made me visit the doctor. And no, I didn't feel any better, but I didn't feel marginally worse. At least now, I was *nearly* convinced that I may have had an illness, and that I wasn't cursed or haunted by some celestial being.

God, that's still mortifying to say. I nearly died when I had to tell the GP. Mam had basically dragged me up to her the day she found me running around the garden in my penguin onesie. After sitting in the waiting for forty minutes, trying to work out what was wrong with everyone else by looking at them, I was finally granted access to Dr. Harper's surgery.

Mam insisted on coming in with me, I don't think she trusted me to reveal the full extent of the problem – which is fair enough, because I had absolutely no intention of telling her anything, I was actually considering faking an ear infection. Not because I didn't want help you see, but I didn't think there was anything they could do. I wouldn't have even minded the mortification of telling her about doing Usain Bolt impressions on the stair case at 5 a.m. if I thought she could fix me. Not being vulgar here, but if a smear test performed by the entirety of blazin' squad could fix me; I would have done that too. I was *DESPERATE.*

Despite my reservations, Dr. Harper wasn't a hippy, she even prescribed me good old-fashioned drugs. She looked at me through wild curly black hair, a bit like a Connemara's answer to Whoopi Goldberg actually, and asked me had I thought of harming myself, or if I was seeing or hearing anything that wasn't there.

I would have laughed at her, if I wasn't so fed up.

No, I didn't want to harm myself, in fact, that's what had me so demented in the first place. I was afraid that something would harm me. No, I wasn't imagining things, and the only voices in my head was my own, and trust me, that was bad enough. The tablets she gave me didn't inspire any great hope, especially as she kept reminding me that it was a low dose. I mean would it have killed her to tell me that these were the strongest/bestest ones you could get?

I was rather surprised that Lacknamon had a mental health centre. The town that I remembered was inhabited by people who were more likely to scorn the local looney, or, if they liked you, say a novena in your honour.

Nowadays, it seemed that Lacknamon was a metropolis for all things holistic and lovely, whodathunkit?

It wasn't just the attitudes to mental health that had changed either. A visit to the town centre with day for one of my appointments was wrought with revelations. Most of Ireland is bankrupt and on the brink of ruin. Lacknamon was like the town that austerity forgot.

New shops had opened; old shops were doing very well. Even horrible ones that sold things like castor oil, kilt making sets, and all sorts of random crap were doing a steady trade.

I asked Dad how the town was doing it.

"Ah sure, we look after our own, and sure nobody here uses the bank anyways, we took all our money out, robbing bastards," he muttered.

Right, I thought ... maybe they were onto something?

When we arrived at our destination, Dad and I exited the car, me for the mad house, Dad for the DIY shop.

"Dad, we need to pay the parking machine, have you change?" I asked.

"Arrah, nobody pays attention to them yokes," he gestured to the meter with scorn.

"But, the parking inspector? You'll be caught, you'll get a ticket," I warned.

"Gerry? Arrah stop, sure he's in there," he gestured to the small pub across the road.

"Gerry Mullins? The local pisshead?" I asked.

"Yeah, they gave him the parking gig when they put up all the metres, he walks around the town all shagging day anyways and it gives him a few pounds for a pint."

Fair enough, I decided and set off.

Like I said, I was surprised to hear that Lacknamon had a mental health centre; I was even more surprised to find that it looked like a bungalow … because it was a bungalow. Rather than purpose building a facility, they had, it seemed renovated a house. Fair do's, I thought, at least it was better than the stocks in the town square I had expected.

After being ushered in, and not made to wait, I was starting to feel optimistic. Incense oil burned with lovely soothing music playing through the whole place, which was warmly lit. I wondered did they have any rooms to rent.

I'm not going to go into the process of what the appointment was like, mainly because not much happened. After a few questions were asked (the same ones the doctor asked me), I was told to lie back, close my eyes and breath. Fair enough, I was instructed how to breath (did you know I had been doing it wrong for YEARS*)*. That was that, all the other visits have basically been the same, breathing, getting prescriptions.

Prescriptions.

Oh how I love thee, let me count the ways!

Sleeping tablets are the bizz, I know, I know, very addictive, blah, blah, blah. But! I was able to sleep now! Now

I don't know if you've ever suffered from sleep deprivation, but I can tell you one thing, I can see why they use it as a torture method. Nights spent tossing and turning, cartwheeling around the bed, counting *fucking sheep*. It was hell. Now though, I had lovely little white tablets of bliss. The other pills I was given were shite though.

When Dr. Ox in Dublin gave me those pills, I had presumed that those were all the psychotropic family had to offer. It seems, however, that those ones were only a short term measure, and I wouldn't be getting them again. What I did get were ones that apparently made no difference in the short-term, but would build up until one day, when I would feel a tiny bit better and might shave my legs or something wild like that.

I was, as you can imagine, less than impressed with that, as I am a spoilt brat with an instant gratification problem. I consulted Dr. Google and suddenly became a wealth of knowledge on SSRIS, anti-depressants, and everything in between. I'd visit the doctor with a list of alternative tablets that might work quicker and every time, get sent away with a flea in my ear, feeling like a smack head.

I'd take my tablet at 4 p.m. each day, now rechristened mad o'clock. I literally counted the hours until it was time to take the next one, hoping that it was like one of those fund raising thermometres, and I would eventually hit the magic number of pills taken, and feel wonderful, for the clouds to list and sunny rays of reality, rationality, and general normality to flood through my psyche. I would have loved to have had a time machine, to fast forward through this horrible stage of limbo. Once, in my desperation, I took four sleeping tablets at once in an attempt to sleep through a few days and be unconscious for a while, to pass the time. All that happened was that I woke up twenty-seven hours later, feeling like I had been on the almighty piss the night before, with a banging headache, my tongue stuck to the roof of my mouth, and the suspicion that the world had ended when I was asleep, like in *28 Days Later*.

For the first week or so that I stayed in my parents' house, I had been granted a temporary amnesty. When I slept for whole days, Mam would just smile and say "Well, you must have needed it, a good sleep and a good laugh, the best cure for anything."

I didn't get away with it for long though, about eight days after I first arrived, she breezed into my room at 8 a.m., with demands to rise and shine. Ever since, I hadn't had bloody *time* to sleep, let alone set up a full-time gloom room. It wasn't just Mam who wouldn't indulge me either. Annie arrived one morning with Oscar who had been sent home early from school for chasing a little girl around the playground with the class goldfish, which had been flapping obscenely and generally mentally scarring his young classmates.

"Why?" I asked him incredulously.

"Because," he explained, "they such wussies, the girls, so me and James thought it would be funny," he told the floor, with pseudo guilty face.

I covered a snigger of laughter. He was really priceless. Wilding adventurous, brutally intelligent, slightly evil, it was bound to get him in trouble.

"Mammy's cross with me, she says she going to send Freddie to boarding school," he whispered.

Freddie was the hamster that had been given to him in place of a radioactive spider.

"She won't, I won't let her, I promise." I squeezed him into a hug.

Chapter 22

After about eight weeks, I fell into a routine. Nothing that could be misconstrued as a life mind you, but a routine for sure. Get up, eat, watch TV with Mam until about four, eat dinner, partake in whatever activity had been planned for the evening in order to "Get me out of the house", eat again, TV, then bed. It wasn't challenging or taxing, or even interesting, but I figured that was what I needed at the minute.

When I had been home for a good while, Mam started to make noises about "Getting me out of the house". I dreaded what this would entail. I was right, so far I had been to yoga classes, creative writing, cake decoration, dog grooming classes with our 15-year-old collie, Ben, who is torn between a desire to bite and hump everything that moves and bingo (which I actually really enjoyed, I won a tenner and a gift voucher for an Easter egg).

The only slight break in the routine was when Annie came round, collected me, and brought me to her house, where I would eat and watch TV there. At first I thought these excursions were out of pity. Annie had two children, I was sure she had better things to do than watch Jeremy Kyle with her looper brained sister. I was wrong though, because it seemed Annie was no longer satisfied with being Susie Homemaker.

"I'm so bored," she confessed one morning.

"All I do is cook and clean, and drive the kids everywhere," she moaned.

"Is there not ... I don't know, like things for people with kids to do? Like support groups?" I asked.

"I have kids, Louise, not a drug problem, I don't need a support group," she scolded.

"Fine, Jesus I dunno, a part-time job maybe?" I asked.

"I've thought about it, I even did a few hours in one of the cafés in town, but they let me go that morning, apparently I have a problem with authority, the cheek of them! I'd say anyone would have a problem with authority if their authority in question was a snotty 17-year-old!" said Annie, with injustice.

Hmm... I considered. Annie probably did have such a problem, along with just a touch of control freakery.

"Or maybe a course? I suggested.

"I don't want to go to school, Jesus, I spend hours doing homework every evening as it is. Ah, I dunno, maybe it'll pass. You're so lucky, you're completely free," she sighed.

Was I? I wondered. Okay, I didn't have anyone relying on me to make their dinner, but I had responsibilities. I had rent to pay (even though I wasn't living there at the moment, I still had to pay it), and at least she had Brian to go to work and bring home the readies, I'd love to sit at home and watch telly, knowing that someone else was paying the cable bill.

I voiced this to her and noticed her eyes bulge with indignity.

"Are you mad? Housekeeping is the hardest job in the world! And there's no thanks! None!" said Annie.

"You sound like Mam," I replied.

"Right, maybe I'll keep looking for a job then," decided Annie, looking a bit freaked out.

Chapter 23

Along with whichever existential crisis Annie was having, I also had Alison calling me on a nearly daily basis, with updates of her and Tony's reproductive systems.

"His sperm is all grand, and so are my hormones, so it's either my plumbing, or it's nothing, and we just have to wait," Alison informed me, early one morning.

"Alison, its eight in the morning, it's a bit early for sperm," I mumbled.

"It's never too early for sperm," said Alison, with a dirty laugh.

"God, you're filthy, and you're going to be someone's mother," I tutted, laughing.

"I hope so anyways, I've to go for some sort of dye test, to make sure there's no blockages or anything, that's on Wednesday, and then *we'll* know." I could hear the excitement in her voice. Whatever floats your boat I Suppose, but it didn't sound like my idea of fun.

"Very good, and is Tony in better form?" I asked.

Tony had apparently been in a proper fouler recently. Alison reckoned it was do with having strangers examining the ins and outs of his bits and pieces.

"No, but never mind him, he'll grow out of it, he's just going through the terrible 28s," she replied, sarcastically.

It wasn't uncommon for Alison and Tony to be at odds these days, but even I had to admit, that it was starting to look serious. Alison seemed to be in complete denial about everything. All she could really think about was having a baby. Baby blinkers, that what she was wearing, I mused. Not long ago, Tony had neglected to return from work, for three days. Alison just happened to mention it in passing while we discussed *X Factor* one morning.

"Three days?!" I asked in shock.

"Yup, he was in Wicklow apparently, getting some *head space!* Head space! I'll give him head space I told him. If I didn't know better I'd say he didn't want this baby," she snapped.

"Are you sure he does?" I asked warily.

"It was his idea!" she replied.

Ah here, that's no way to carry on, I thought.

"Maybe he's just getting it all out of his system, before you do get knocked up, being wild and young and free?" I suggested.

"Hmm, maybe," Alison replied, but she didn't sound convinced. I didn't blame her.

"Maybe you should take off for a few days, come visit me, I'm bored off my tricycle here, and I promise, I'm actually feeling a good bit better, I won't set fire to anything," I laughed.

"Are you really? You sound better, less monosyllabic," said Alison.

Am I really? Well ... yes, I suppose, I thought. I didn't know if it was the fact that I had very little time to wallow in self-pity and obsession, or maybe it was the pills *finally* working, but, yeah, I felt a small bit better. Not the same as I had been, but less... despairing, as I had only weeks ago.

"Sure I do, sure I'm grand, now, come visit me and we can drink wine and watch *Footloose*," I offered, I had a thing about Kevin Bacon, he made me itchy, isn't he just *vile?!* Alison, however, loved him. Maybe he was the celebrity version of marmite, or marzipan.

"Fuck it, I will, I'm due a couple of days off work anyways, I'll take the weekend off, will I pack me good wellies?" she asked, suspiciously.

As a Dubliner, Alison was highly suspicious of the countryside. I'm pretty sure she envisioned a barren, hilly backwater, which in all fairness was far from the truth these days; Lacknamon even had a nightclub now. I can't imagine it was any great shakes, but it was a start.

I hate to admit, but, I think I was starting to *like living here.*

It was tranquil enough to be a relief from Dublin, but with all the amenities close by, even a recently developed road connected us to Cork city with only a forty minute drive in between.

"Hahaha, you can if you want, but you'll be the only one wearing them, all the auld wans down here are wearing Manlolo Blahniks since they discovered net a porter," I informed her.

"You're messing, d'ya member the last time I was there? What was it? Three years ago? And that mad hick laughed at my coat?" she asked indignantly.

I did remember, it was a seven hundred euro coat, fresh off the catwalks, it turned more than a few heads in Tully's, the local drinking hole, though.

"It's not like that anymore, I promise, you could wear your spangly bikini down the main street and you'd probably start a trend, its great!" I enthused.

"God, you've changed your tune," she mused.

"Yes," I agreed, I had.

Chapter 24

What was that noise? I wondered sleepily ... it was getting louder. Was my head shaking? It fucking was. Jesus, what was going on? Was it an earthquake? I sat up quickly and the room spun. Uuugghhh, God.

I was *dying*.

Alison had been in Lacknamon one night so far and my liver had been pickled. Last night we decided to brave the bright lights of Lacknamon's Friday night scene. For hours, Alison, Annie and I pranced around my bedroom, like teenagers trying on clothes, doing makeup, drinking and dancing, the usual getting ready routine. The only problem was that by the time we were ready to go, Annie was a little worse for wear. I wondered if we would have a problem getting her into the nightclub, and then I remembered this was Lacknamon, not New York, they probably had wheelchairs for this exact problem, ones that were chained to the bar.

With Annie singing "Girls just wanna have fun", and Alison talking about oestrogen and ovulation tests, a very red faced dad drove us into town. It reminded me of the good old days. I even had to tap Dad for cash on exiting the car, and had him warn us all about behaving ourselves. I actually enjoyed it. I felt minded. Ask Freud about *that one,* cos' I hadn't a clue.

Onwards to the obligatory pub crawl. Now, I hadn't been out in Lacknamon in a very long time, I hadn't a clue where to go. All I knew was that there were about ten pubs to every one person, so one of them had to be okay.

The first pub, was a mistake. When we entered, I swear it went silent, and beady eyes followed us to our seats. When we did get to sit down, as noisily and awkwardly as possible, none of us wanted to get back up, for fear of causing yet more consternation.

"*You* go!" I elbowed Alison, giggling.

"*FUCK off, you go!*" she replied.

"Ah here, I'll go, yeh big girls," said Annie, wobbily standing, glassy-eyed.

We watched her wobble to the bar, and impressively order drinks with the confidence that only a woman on her tenth vodka possesses.

I almost expected the barman to refuse her. "We don' lak strangers here in dese parts," with a southern drawl, but no, sure enough, she tottered back with drinks, quickly enough.

"Right, we'll finish these quickly, and leave," I instructed, trying not to laugh.

"Stop, it's like a MORTUARY in here! The feckin' hills DO have eyes," screeched Annie, laughing.

Err yeah ... I replied, noticing that everyone in the pub had looked up at us. Christ, there goes our crops this year.

So, with Annie humming the theme song to deliverance, we headed off and low and behold, we were much more successful in our next pub.

This time, Alison steered Annie to a quiet corner, while I fetched the drinks. I say "fetched" as if I did it with any speed, but it seemed that the whole of Ireland was wedged into this particular pub. I noticed a band playing at the back, and figured that was what had attracted the crowds. I had no idea of knowing though, because I couldn't hear them playing music over the raucous crowd.

Elbowing my way to the bar, I finally reached it, with the minimal of warm beer spilt on my shoulders and dress. I stood doing a sort of Mexican wave at the barman, a young good-looking type, who caught my eye, acknowledged me and then went off to check his appearance in the mirror in the gents. Ah yes, that's about right.It was all coming back to me now.

A short while later, an old ungood-looking type took mine and about thirty other people's orders, which he mixed up completely and I, of course, was too polite to say.

"Whadda fuck is this?" demanded Annie.

"Sherry, now shut up and drink it," I replied.

"Fair do's. What have you got, Alison?" Annie asked.

"Warm Port and lemon? I think." She winced as she tried it.

"No harm, good for a cold that is," I commented, whilst sipping my crème de menthe and thinking of the poor flu riddled man at the bar, looking confusedly at his vodka and Red Bull.

We drank heavily, and soon became loud. As the night progressed, we became famous in the pub as the girls with the mad drinks.

"We're eccentric millionaires," Alison told a crowd of 18 year-olds from Cork. "We drink these things because their classy." She hiccupped.

We were soon on first name terms with the bar staff, and after a while, became obnoxious, due to our newfound popularity. When our drinks needed refilling, or we needed nuts of crisps, we would simply press a tenner at one of the youths, who would run off to the bar and come back with more and more outlandish drinks.

On the way to the "nightclub" we teamed up with a crowd of hens, who had brought along a young niece of about eighteen, and later that night, I'm pretty sure she was found weeping incoherently, having drank a Cointreau and Gin Cocktail invented by Annie.

The following morning was not all that great altogether.

There was a herd of elephants doing the cancan somewhere, and it was getting louder. I slowly peeled Alison off my legs and stepped out of bed. A loud grunt came from the floor, where Annie was asleep on a mostly deflated air mattress with the majority of her head in a (thankfully empty) sick basin. I had stepped on her.

"Ooof, sorry, Annie," I apologised.

She grunted. Apology accepted I reckon.

Poor Annie, we lost her somewhere in the nightclub, only to get a text from Mam saying that she had been delivered home by a group of young lads on push bikes.

I carried on through the house, following the noise, which got louder and louder.

I swung the front door open, to find three men apparently digging up the front garden.

"Waddafuckerrdewin?!" I asked eloquently, blinded by the sun.

"Waterworks," came a gruff reply.

I responded by giving them each a filthy look, when I noticed that one of them was the good-looking type barman from last night. I nearly hissed at them.

"Humph." I closed the door and went off to find water.

Noticing my reflection in one of the many mirrors that Mam had placed all over the house, I cringed inwardly. The good-looking barman had seen me like *this*?

Not good. My eye makeup was swimming around my chin, my hair was defying gravity up one side of my head, and the dress that had looked fabulous last night, was crumpled to feck. My eyes were a fetching pink colour, yet my lips were lined in a lovely plum, from the port I think.

Moans and groans indicated that my Alison and Annie had also gotten up. I met them in the kitchen with Mam.

"Like a drunken teenager, you were, and you a married woman with two children," I heard Mam, poor Annie.

"Did you ever hear the like of it, getting a *backie* off a gang of lads on push bikes, eating chips and singing ... if that's what you could *call* it," she carried on.

"How's the head?" I asked Annie.

"Ah, stop, I've the fear – the terrible feary fear, was I as bad as I remember?" she asked.

"Nooo, of course not, you were lovely," I lied.

"Liar ... Thanks though," she replied.

The three of us spent the rest of the day, lying around the house, demanding fizzy drinks and new release films.

"Oooh, this is the *life!*" cheered Annie, laying on the couch, eating chips. She was enjoying some temporary release this weekend, leaving Brian to mind the children.

"I might move home myself," she joked.

"You will not," butted in Mam. "Get your slippers off the sofa," she scolded.

Chapter 25

The waterworks carried on all weekend, and the more I noticed the good-looking type barman, the more my interest grew. God, he was gorgeous-looking.

I was like a skittery young one running around the house, trying to catch a glimpse of him through the windows. It wasn't just me – Alison and Annie, and to some extent Mam, we're fascinated by him.

"He looks like Channing Tatum," breathed Alison.

"Only Irish, Channing Tayto!" said Mam.

"Fuck, he's looking, hide!" I giggled.

All four of us we're crowded at the sitting room window, peeking behind the curtain at him.

I dared to peek again, and, of course, he caught me. A sly wink from him with a clearly self-satisfied grin, and he carried on with his work.

"Oh my god!" Annie thrilled.

"He fancies Louise," Mam singsonged.

"Mam, he does not, and don't say fancy, you're too old," I rebutted, shyly, blushing.

"I am not! And he *does!* I went out this morning with tea for them, and he didn't even give me a look," she said, almost bitterly.

"And you a married woman," said Annie, quite cattily.

"But this is brilliant, if you go out and get the ride off him, well then, you'll be grand, how could you not be?" Alison said.

"Ah here, I'm going out, *behave yourselves*, no 'getting the ride'," said Mam, clearly embarrassed.

Before she could walk off tutting and calling Alison vulgar, the doorbell went.

We all looked at each other, thinking the same thing ... it's not? Is it?

"It is! Mam, you go! Louise, c'mere till we fix your hair," Annie commanded.

"He won't even want to see me, they probably want to turn off the water again, relax." I wasn't keen on the idea of actually interacting with him, I don't know why, but it made me nervous.

"Just in case, be prepared," she said.

"Yes, brown owl," I answered, smartly, whilst she pulled a brush through my hair and Alison smeared lip balm onto me.

I noticed Mam straightening her apron and pouffing up her curls, so did Alison and Annie. She caught us grinning and scolded, "You three have filthy minds." You couldn't blame her though.

We heard her doing her "Posh voice" which made her sound like Graham Norton while they tried to ascertain which lady he was calling upon.

"Oh, dark hair? You must mean Louise, I'll just get her for you," she simpered.

"No! No! Tell him I'm not in!" I panicked.

"How can I do that? He saw you gawking at him out the window," she pointed out.

"Oh Jesus," I sighed, feeling sick I approached the bench ... I mean the front door.

"Hi, Louise, is it?" he asked, with his beautiful mouth.

"Yeah," I replied, well tried to, but my voice had gone all high-pitched and stupid. I cleared my throat, which turned into a phlegmy hacking cough. I shouldn't be allowed out I deduced.

"I, ehh, noticed you and your friends, looking out the window earlier, and well, I especially noticed you." He leaned sideways against the door frame, closer to me.

"Oh, yeah, well you're doing great work out there, the water will be ehh ... good and runny," I answered. *Runny?* Like diarrhoea? Was I for real?

"Yeah ... emm, look, would you like to come out, with me? One of the nights? Maybe the pictures or something? You can pick the film!" He smiled.

"Oh, emm," I considered, still puce with embarrassment over runny. "I don't think so, Channing," I started.

"Eoin," he intercepted.

"Of course! Eoin, yeah, sorry. It's just I do be very busy of an evening, helping Mam and stuff. Sorry though." I smiled, I just wasn't able for someone as good-looking as him, I'd probably be so nervous next time I'd start discussing ingrown toenails.

"She will of course! Sure, don't be silly, Louise, I'm grand, I don't need help! What night? Monday suit you? Lovely! She'll see you Monday, eight o'clock?" Mam directed.

Channing/Eoin *looked* at me; I registered no complaint (I was in shock at being pimped out by Mam) and then agreed.

"Eight o'clock, I'll collect you." He nodded slowly. Clearly amused, I didn't blame him.

When the door was closed, Mam rounded on me.

"Louise Patricia Casey, are you simple or what? 'No, I have to help me mammy', you big thick, even I know that sounds stupid, and *of course* you want to go out with him! Are you blind?" she admonished me.

"I know! I know I do, I panicked! I cannot believe you though!" I said, still bewildered by what had just happened.

"Well, someone had to step in," she said. "Now, we have a lot to do before Monday night, a lot to do," she said, eyeing my grimly.

Chapter 26

Monday night at 7:30 p.m., Mam, Annie, even *Dad* and Alison who refused to leave until I got back from my date, all sat on my bed having helped me choose an outfit, made me apply all sorts of gunk to my skin, and then mentally prepared me for my date. By "mentally prepared" I mean they had sat me down and made me memorise topics of conversation.

"If we left it to you'd start on about runny water again!" Alison snickered.

"Oh stop, I won't even be able to look at him!" I lamented.

"You will, now stop; right again, what is good to talk about?" asked Annie.

"Football, the weather (but not for long), music, work, and ehh ... oh god I've forgotten," I said.

"Holidays!" Piped Oscar, who had also been roped in to help ready me.

"Good man, yes, travel, *okay*, I know them now," I declared.

"And what do you not talk about?" asked Mam, sternly.

"Runny ... water, bodily functions, Michael Bublé, how much I hate Kevin Bacon and Jeremy Kyle," I answered, confidently.

"By Jove, I think she's got it," cracked Mam, but kindly.

At five to eight, the doorbell rang.

"He's *keen*," remarked Oscar, who had gotten wrapped up in the girly atmosphere.

"Here goes," I announced, took a deep breath and slipped on my coat.

Well, actually, Annie's coat, as I still hadn't got many clothes, just the basics that Mam got in Primark and a few warm bits from the winter. I really must arrange to call Amanda and see if she would send some of my stuff down, but that was a whole other story, we'll get to that later.

I breathed deeply again, and opened the door. I nearly hit the deck when I was reminded of how devastatingly gorgeous he was.

"Hi, ready to go?" Eoin asked, and nodded towards his car, which was also a fairly gorgeous Landrover, about the same size as my flat in Dublin.

"Yeah, definitely, let's go," I replied, eager to escape my family who were listening in the hallway, before Mam could come out and offer my hand in marriage.

I walked silently to the car, shite, silence, that's not good.

"Cold night isn't it?" I remarked.

"Wha? Oh yeah, it is, emm, Louise? Why is there a woman holding a bag of crisps at the window?" he asked, perplexed.

I looked back, and sure enough, Alison was waving a multi-pack of Tayto at us, breaking her bollox laughing.

"Oh, ermm, she's not well in the head, don't mind her," I dismissed, I'd kill her.

Following all the rules, I actually managed to keep up a steady stream of conversation, the whole way to the cinema, I breezed through topics. Which is more than could be said for Eoin, who would occasionally threw in the occasional "Mmm? Is that right?" and "God, I don't know". I was beginning to doubt that he was the full all-rounder that I had once thought.

When we arrived at the cinema, would you believe, he jumped out of the car, ran round, and opened my door. My heart melted, I didn't care if he was a bit slow, he was *adorable!*

I did in fact, pick the movie. A comedy about a man with cancer, I couldn't handle any of the smaltzy rom-coms that were on offer or the testosterone fests, so it seemed like a good middle ground.

Now, I'm not being shallow, I'm really not, but, well, I don't think Eoin really, *got* the film. Like, when the protagonist made jokes about his illness, everyone else know it was *sarcasm*. Eoin, on the other hand, was horrified, "That's terrible," he exclaimed at one point. "You can't shave off your hair to keep your toes warm!"

I was a little bit mortified when the couple in front us laughed at him, in fact I wanted to get up and leave. He just wouldn't shut up! It was worse than watching a director's commentary. "Who's that fella? Is he not the doctor from earlier? No, well he looks an awful lot like him!"

I truly felt for him, but it was pity, not empathy, and having said that, I felt sorry for me, too.

He tried to hold my hand, but grabbed my wrist. Completely unfussed by this, he then went to put an arm across my shoulders and elbowed me in the ear.

He settled at resting his hand on my forearm and I relaxed to watch the movie, nursing my poor ear.

It was only when the girl from the other couple looked around after Eoin noted that the female lead looked like Mila Kunis (She *was Mila Kunis)* that she noticed that Eoin was drop dead gorgeous, I noticed the surprise register on her face, then the envy. That's right you cow! Ha! See, he's a fine thing; he doesn't need to know anything! Chuffed, I decided to hold his hand. Unfortunately, he got the same idea and I ended up with a whole cup of icy lemonade on my lap.

After the movie, looking like I'd wet myself in my lovely designer jeans (Annie would kill me) the subject of "Sooo, what now?" came up.

I was sorely tempted. He was gorgeous, but, in all honestly, I couldn't bring myself to fancy him anymore. I mean I'm not blind, I could still see the physical appeal, but I didn't fancy him any more than I fancied a photograph of him, nice to look at, but no depth. I'm not saying that I only ever go for Stephen Hawking types, but when he got excited that someone in the credits had the same first name as him, I had to draw the line.

"Actually, I'm pretty wrecked, I think I'll head home," I said, fake yawning.

"Oh, okay," said Eoin, clearly disappointed. I suppose he didn't get rejected very often.

Back in the car, I started to regret my decision to hasten home, especially when I noticed his shoulder muscles ripple as he closed his door.

Would I make up my mind?

I decided to go on the offensive, to see if there was any hope at all.

Maybe I was just asking the wrong questions, bringing up the wrong topics, and who was I to judge? As mentioned before, I was hardly a MENSA candidate myself.

"So, Eoin, do you watch any telly? I'm gone mad into Jeremy Kyle myself at the minute, it's hilarious, all the fights and that." Woops, broke a rule, but feck it.

"Ah yeah, it's good fun, there's one thing I never get though, why don't the women ever have to take DNA tests to see is the baby is *theirs?!*" he asked.

Oh Christ ... never mind.

Part 2

Chapter 27

<u>Two Months later</u>

The June sun pounded onto the pavements that click-clacked against my high heels. Yup, I was running in heels again. I had a meeting with a bank manager at two o'clock, it was now gone five past and I wasn't even nearly ready.

I walked past Lacknamon Post Office and broke into a run, I couldn't be late for this, I don't mean to exaggerate, but this could be the most important meeting of my life.

I ran past the run-down stone clad building that had been occupying my every thought for the last month. The old stained glass sky lights reflecting blues and purples on the shop floor, visible through a huge window at the front. I closed my eyes for a second and wished, as hard as I could. *Please, please, please!*

Sorry, I'll catch you up!

I had a meeting with the bank to see about getting a loan. A loan to open a shop. In Lacknamon. A home wares shop. In Lacknamon.

The idea came to me just after my disastrous date with Eoin. I sat at home for a few days, bemoaning my failure. What was I doing with my life? After starting to feel better, I should really start revising my plan of becoming the simpleton daughter living in my parents back bedroom until the day I died.

The prospect of spending every day, following a strict television schedule of Jeremy Kyle, Bonanza, and Dr. Quinn medicine woman with my mother every day forever made my eyes water. And I'd been doing enough crying recently.

It was Annie who sparked the idea actually.

Once again, I was sat in her kitchen, listening to her complain about how bored she was with everything.

"If only I could be my own boss," she whined. "Or a manager or something! But I'm not good at anything," she despaired.

"Yes you are, look how fabulous this house is, it's gorgeous! You've done this! Maybe you could take up interiors, but you'd have to do a course of something," I cheered.

"Nah, I'm too busy with the kids, she backtracked.

Annie may have thought that was an innocent conversation, but she had sparked an idea. Maybe I could be my own boss? But doing what? What was I good at? I needed to do something, especially in light of the fact that I had literally no money left.

I stewed on the idea for a few days, until, in a fit of boredom, I decided to clean the house, which was already spotless. It was while I was dusting underneath millions of Mam's frankly hideous ornaments, that it hit me. I like houses, doing them up I mean. I could ... I could have a shop! Where I sold things for people to put in their houses. Okay, I wasn't going to change the world, but I could try being happy, couldn't I?

Only, I had no money. I also knew nothing about business except that it required a lot of typing and coffee on my part. It was then that I approached Dad, who thought it was a great idea, and Annie, who wanted in.

Only she had no spare cash either, as they had just put an extension on their already massive house.

It was Mam who suggested we try the bank, after I declined Dad's offer of a loan. I didn't feel right, I wanted to try and do this without bankrupting my parents. If it went belly-up and the bank was left short-changed, I could live with that, in fact I might even take some satisfaction on behalf of the rest of the country. I couldn't do it to my parents though.

That was why this meeting was so important. I needed capital, and fast; especially as I had already located an ideal premises. The stone clad shop with the stained glass skylights. I sighed when I thought of it. It was perfect. I don't know if you remember me saying how I felt like I was under water before, but this was the same, only nice. Even on dull grey days, light was transformed in the little shop, which would be full of blues and greens and purples, dancing in the light of the sun-rays. I found the shop whilst wandering about the town, looking for Starbucks (yes, in Lacknamon, I couldn't believe it either). It poked out behind a large book shop, just catching my eye and I had to have a look.

Apparently, it had once been a monk's cell, as part of the ruined monastery that had once stood behind the church, then butchers, then a clothes shop, and now it stood empty, as it had for five years. The rent on it was tiny, so it wouldn't even be an expensive startup; I just need stock and some money to get going.

I had a delicately prepared business plan that would put Bill Cullen to shame (courtesy of Dad), I had revised for this meeting more times that I ever did for my leaving cert exams and I had so much hope. Something I never thought I would have again.

My phone beeped. A text from Annie,

Break a leg! Counting on u, much love A xx

No pressure then. Annie was going to be an employee, she decided. She didn't have the time of the inclination to be involved in starting the business, but she did like the sound of helping out, and apparently, if I, as her boss annoyed her, she could at least tell me to feck off without getting fired. I already suspected problems, but no need to say anything yet.

Phone beeped again.

Good luck, honey! I believe in u! Al xxx

Bless, she had gone through so much in last few months, the subject of which I simply *must* tell you about soon!

Oooh, at the bank, back in a minute.

Chapter 28

Poor Alison. They say it never rains but it pours, they were right.

On the day that Alison went for her dye test, she got two surprises.

One was that Tony never showed. He had promised and promised that he would be there; she had even made him write it down. Alison's confidence in him had seemingly been badly knocked by his impromptu holiday to Wicklow, and she sensed that he was having second thoughts. Rather than ask him about this, she was choosing to ignore and plough on full steam ahead. All through the weekend that she had visited me in Lacknamon, I prayed and prayed that he wouldn't let her down.

At the clinic that day, Alison delayed her appointment for a full hour before finally admitting defeat.

"I wasn't even going to go in for the test, only it was paid for already, and like a big thick, I was still hoping that he was stuck in traffic, even though he wasn't answering his phone," she cried and sobbed to me that night on the phone.

Alison went in for the test, and before they even approached her with dye or whatever it was they planned to use, they decided a little *ahem* examination was in order.

Oh the joys of womanhood.

Alison laid there, legs in the air (her words, not mine) and wondered what was going on when she noticed the doctor furrow his brow, he muttered to the nurse and apparently she had a good auld root around in Alison's plumbing, too.

She was pregnant.

"Well I nearly fell off the bed," she told me. "Pregnant? I says, what are ya on about? I am not, that's why I'm here," she objected.

"Honestly, Lou, it was like telling a man that he was pregnant, I just didn't believe them. We'd been trying for so long!" she exclaimed.

"How far gone are you?" I asked.

"Not long, only about twelve weeks, but still, I should have noticed," she blurted out.

"I was so embarrassed, how could I not have noticed? They must have thought I was a right eejit," she almost laughed, then started to cry.

See, another part of Alison's big surprise, was waiting for her at home.

When she burst through the door of her house, full of good news, expecting Tony to be there, with a broken leg and a "Bloody good explanation", she found instead a note on the table, addressed to her.

"He's left me, the fuckin' bastard left me!" she started, when I answered the call that night.

"Oh, emm, *hello*," I cheered.

"Not hello, I'm after gettin' dumped! And I'm pregnant! Jesus, I'm like white trash!" she whined.

Since then, Alison had refused to speak to Tony, who still it seemed wanted to be apart from her, but was awfully sorry about his timing.

"I didn't know she was pregnant," he pleaded with me on the phone. "She didn't even know for feck sake! Will you get her to call me, Louise? Please?" he begged.

"I will not, you made your bed, lie in it," I snapped. The cheek of him, I knew where my loyalty was, thank you very much.

When I told Alison that he had called me, she didn't seem surprised. "He also rang my ma, my da, and my two sisters, he even rang *Amanda!*" she told me, and then fell silent. Touchy Subject.

I had tried to contact Amanda so many times since returning to my parents' house. Through text, by phoning her, I even asked Alison to visit her and see if she could get through to her. It seemed that Amanda wanted breathing space from me for the minute.

It was awful. She told Alison that after my little "Episode" and burning down the kitchen and all the palaver that went with it, she didn't feel able to deal with me at the minute. I didn't blame her to be honest, but it still hurt. I had come through so much recently, my life was finally starting to come together somewhat, and now this. Amanda seemed to be the one casualty of my illness, and I would have preferred to have lost a leg.

For the first day or so, after I had found out that she didn't want anything to do with me anymore, I was heartbroken. It was like losing my job all over again. Everything seemed so *pointless*. I remembered all of the best things about living with her. The time she had spotted Mrs Upstairs coming out of Mikhals flat at 3 a.m., looking flushed and we had wolf whistled at her. How she would ring in sick for me if I had a hangover, then stay home too and we would watch crappy TV all day and eat ice cream. It was like losing a lover, only much worse. She had been one of my best friends.

It was Mam who snapped me out of my heartbreak. "Jesus, get out of that bed, I'm not wasting all these months of driving you in and out the mad house, and the price of those tablets and seeing you so miserable again, Amanda will get over it, and if she doesn't, then so what? That's life, you can't take to the bed like a Jane Austen character every time you have a fight with one of your pals, you'll get bed sores, and what's more, you'll get a kick in the arse from me," she snapped one morning, pulling the duvet away from me.

I knew she was right, and what's more I wouldn't put it past her not to deliver that kick, so I got up, arranged an appointment at the mental health clinic and dusted myself off. It still hurt though.

Chapter 29

Back to my Bank managers meeting. Well, I sat down in a squeaky brown chair and waited for the MC to arrive.

I was like a prize fighter, all reared up and ready for my showdown.

A very short Danny De Vito looking fella came in; wearing what looked like a communion suit.

"Well, now, Mizz Ehh, Cassseey izz it?" he asked, in a really irritating nasal voice.

"Yes, Mr De vit – Mr Hammond, that's me," I replied, quickly.

Fuck.

"It's a small business loan you're looking for, izz it?" he asked, again with the stupid voice.

"That's right, if you'll look here you'll see I have my business plan laid out for you clearly, along with projected profits and a feasibility study, if you'd like some time to go through, I can sit here quietly or I could come back, whichever is easiest." I smiled as pleasantly as I could manage, although I seemed to have taken a strong disliking to him.

"Yah, roish, I see, hmm, well I've taken the liberty of looking through your personal accounts, which seem to be overdrawn quite badly, can you offer any explanation for that?" he quizzed, as though he had found a dead body in my boot, not an overdraft.

"Well, yes, I do realise that my personal accounts aren't as healthy as they could be, but I was recently unwell and returned to the area to my parents –" I started.

"Unwell?!" he asked, and stepped away slightly.

"Don't worry, nothing contagious." I fake laughed girlishly, fuckhead.

"Yes, well, even so, I'm afraid that in light of your current personal financial affairs, you just wouldn't be what we're looking for at the minute for a small business loan, in fact, we are going to have to start seeing some activity in your personal accounts quite soon, and I do mean some income by that," he chortled, and I resisted the urge to fling a stapler at his head.

"And you couldn't have mentioned this on the phone? When I called for this appointment? Or after you had looked at the business plan? Do you know what, Mr Hammond, you're an arsehole!" I informed him, quietly.

"Well now, Oi think that's unnecessary, Mizzz Casssey –" he flustered.

"Ah shove it," I dismissed, and walked out.

I was livid; I'd never been more insulted. Overdraft, what feckin' overdraft, it was a couple of hundred on one card, and what's more, I had only taken it out yesterday, to pay for the stupid suit that I was now wearing.

I was nearly in tears when I finally landed home, and like the big baby that I had become, I told my mammy on him.

"Well now, the cheek of him! I've a right mind to go down there and tell him what he can do with his overdraft!" she spluttered.

"It won't make any difference, I'm screwed, there's nothing I can do – the shops off," I said, quietly.

"It is not! Louise Casey, when did I ever raise you to be such a defeatist? We'll sort the money, you can let your dad help you for a start, and I won't take no for an answer, we trust you, pet, and what's more, we want to help, nothing would make your father and I happier than to see you succeed and be happy. Take the lend, pet, besides, we know where you live," she joked.

"Oh, Mam, I don't know what to say, you've both been so good to me, I couldn't –" I shook my head.

"Yes, you could, and what's more, you will, I was only thinking the last day, sure you never had a 21st, or an 18th, and we never went further than Kerry for a holiday because your father won't fly, so we've already saved loads of money on you," she explained, as if that completely justified them lending me thousands of euros.

"Your mother is right, and what's more, you'll be a great success, so we'll make our money back, you're a great bet! We'll be able to retire on you!" Dad chipped in.

I snivelled a little more, and then swallowed ... "Are you ... sure? I'll pay you back, every cent! With interest! I'll work so hard, and make you both so proud, I promise," I said.

I had a lot to prove, and not just to my parents, to myself. I had spent the guts of the last six months thinking myself useless, unworthy and crap. It was time to prove myself wrong.

Chapter 30

From the moment that Mam and Dad offered to lend me the money, it was non-stop work. I had so many ideas, which surprised me as I had unable to see past my own misery for so long.

Even without the shop, I was in constant demand. Alison, was into her fourth month of pregnancy and apparently "Sick as a dog". She was also still refusing to speak to Tony, and more than once I had been on the phone in the middle of the night, listen to my friend sob and fret about her situation.

"I'll have to quit work, I can't work in a pub while I'm pregnant, the baby will be born drunk on fumes, singing stupid pop songs, and then I'll have no money, oh god, Louise, what am I going to do?" she asked, despairingly.

I really wished I had answers for her, truly, but I was worse than useless. I told her to come back to Lacknamon for a while, to take compassionate leave from work which she had already been offered, but I think it was down to the fact that she had to abandon the bar for a good puke every twenty minutes.

"I can't, I have to work, and besides, I'm hoping that Tony will come back," she mumbled.

"But, Alison, if you want him back, why don't you just ring him? Sort things out?" I asked.

"Because, he hasn't actually said to anyone that that's what he wants, and I refuse to be the one to make the first move, and he can feck off if he thinks he's hiding behind a phone, I want him in front of me, so I can kick him in the goolies," she spoke, with a hint of malice.

"Okay, Okay, well, I don't know what to do, I mean, if you and Tony don't make it up, then it will be fine, plenty of women have babies alone, and they're perfectly happy, too, but we'll just have sort something out with your work, don't worry, we'll sort it together," I promised. I'd never forget how she had looked after me when I needed it, and I'd be damned if I was going to let her down now.

"Thanks, Lou, *you're* a pal. Go on, I'll let you go back to sleep, I've got to and dry heave for a few hours, night," she said, and rang off.

It seemed that I barely closed my eyes when Mam woke me. "Here, post for you, and you might want to consider getting up a decent hour now that you're going to be a business woman, I'm not your maid you know!" she bellyached.

"Yeah, sorry, getting up now," I told the pillow that my face was buried in.

I unpeeled my head from the pillow and flicked through the post. Mostly junk mail, until I came across a handwritten envelope.

If this is from Kevin, I thought, I'm going back to sleep. I opened it and recognised Amanda's writing.

Louise,

I'm sorry, I'm so, so sorry. I'm writing you a letter because I'm too ashamed to call or text, even as I write this I know I'm going to be up the wall waiting for a reply, hoping that you'll forgive me for being such a cow.

I didn't mean to cut you out. I'm just no good at dealing with the issues you had. I'm so glad to hear that you're doing better. I want you to know why I acted like I did. You're not the first person I've seen go under like that. Someone close to me had the same problem, my sister. Laura had depression from the day she was born until the day she took her own life, and seeing you suffer the same way, it was too hard for me. It brought back too many memories, and I had to escape.

I hope that you will be able to find it in your heart to forgive me, but I'll understand if you can't be my friend anymore. I'll send your stuff on as soon as you want, just let me know.

Amanda

Oh…

Chapter 31

I watched the progress in the shop with amazement, every time I visited it, the builders had added something new for me to marvel at. A new shelf? Oh my god, I was thrilled! A door frame? Janey mac, that's brilliant.

I was so proud of how it was coming together, and oh, the hours of fun I had picking stock. It was like shopping, but on a grander scale and for other people. Amanda came to see the progress; I called her as soon I had finished the letter. A long and tearful call later and it was as if the last few months had never happened.

Interesting development, Colm the Guard, had been to the flat looking for me. Apparently, he had brought round lots of victim support information. Amanda spotted his cute little face and decided that she was having him. Apparently, they had frequented every night club in Dublin and he was doing much better these days. I was glad about that. To be honest, I had forgotten about him. It had been so long since I had allowed myself to think about the mugging, it almost felt like it had happened to someone else.

I no longer cared about Mugger man; he could feck off for himself. The prick...

I, instead, busied myself with shop. So many things to consider: mainly, what to call it. Page after page in my notebook was full of ideas, but they weren't right.

Annie and I slaved over cups of tea thinking of names, honestly, it was worse than naming a child.

"Think, it has to be something that describes what you sell, but not something stupid like 'fancy yokes for your gaff'," said Annie, slurping coffee.

"We're going to sell things ... for the home, bits and bobs?" I suggested.

"That's overdone," Mam interjected. "I know! Bits of Home? How's that?" she suggested, brightly.

"God, Mam, you're brilliant! I love it! What about you, Annie? What do you think?" I asked.

"It's perfect," she smiled.

My phone buzzed away in my bag, I checked to see who was calling, it was Alison.

"He wants a divorce," she spoke quietly. "I'm three months pregnant and he wants a divorce ..."

"Is it not a bit soon? I thought those things took ages?" I asked.

"Sorry, a petition for divorce, same bloody thing though!" She sounded hysterical

I'm on my way," I spoke, sounding more confident than I felt.

Chapter 32

I knew I had to go back to Dublin when Alison rang. She needed me and I owed her. The mark of a true friend was someone who could be there when you weren't at your best, and Alison had been a true friend and more to me when I was feeling like I was less than dirt.

I told Mam and Dad that I was going back.

"Just for a visit!" I told their appalled faces. "I'll be back before the end of the month, there's still so much to do for the opening. I just want to visit Alison and get the rest of my stuff from the flat, that's all. Don't worry, I'm fine," I assured them gently.

"Your father will drive you on Saturday, you could be back and all by Saturday night!" suggested Mam. Dad looked affronted at his services being offered for the trip, still haunted by last time I imagine.

"No, I'll get the train, I just need a lift to the station," I hinted, like a teenager.

The following day I found myself in a large queue on the train. Twenty or so passengers were walking backwards down a carriage as the catering trolley had decided to block the aisle. We waited beside the toilets for half an hour while the trolley served all the seated passengers their teas, coffees, and soggy sandwiches.

After the trolley had passed, I found the seat that I had pre-booked, gently removed the Spanish tourists from it and sat down. I rested my newspaper ... okay, my copy of Hello on the little fold down table, and it immediately stuck to the sticky little surface. I regretted my decision to go via train very, very much.

Forty or so blissful minutes passed and I couldn't believe my good fortune, would I really be allowed to sit alone? A whole foot of space, just for me?

We arrived at the first stop and I held my breath until we set off again. Still nobody in the seat beside me ... did I dare dream?

Suddenly, forty Tesco carrier bags swung into the seat, swiftly followed by a woman of about sixty. She smiled beatifically at me. "Hello, loveen, do you mind if I just squeeze in here? The train is packed!" she shouted at me.

I was tempted to tell her that I needed the space for my colostomy bag, which had just leaked, but then my conscience beat my even side into submission.

"No, no, it's fine, let me just make room for your... groceries," I replied, dully.

"Oh, what's that you're reading? I do love the stories in them magazines!" she thrilled, after depositing herself into her seat after much kerfuffle.

"*The Satanic Verses*," I replied, hoping for quiet.

"Oooh, I see ... c'mere, is that like that *Fifty Shades of Grey*?" she whispered.

The rest of the journey was uneventful, after trying and failing to feed me seventy ham sandwiches (which, in fairness were delicious), I parted ways with Maureen, (we were now close friends on a first name basis), and got the bus to my old flat. The familiarity of everything: the streets, the buildings, even the buses, a much missed amenity, should have been comforting. Despite all my therapy and pills, I found them unsettling, but I managed to keep calm all the way to my old flat.

It was empty when I arrived, which made me sad. It was after six in the evening, which meant Amanda should have been home.

I went to my room, which smelt, felt and looked like the haven of safety I had made it into before I had left.

An hour later, I was still packing like billio, flinging things into boxes and bags. My newfound peace of mind had replaced my attention to detail and organisational skills, a small price to pay, of course.

I heard the front door opening and fought the urge to rush out and greet Amanda, I figured she wouldn't want to see me and I didn't want to make it awkward. I had already decided to take a taxi to Alison's and stay there tonight, after leaving my last month's rent and sneaking out of here like a thief in the night.

"Is she here? Helloooo, Louise?!" came Alison's voice.

Confused I called back.

"I'm in my room, what are you doing here?" I asked, as she appeared in the doorway.

Before she could answer, I ran to her and enveloped her into a bone crushing hug. I was so pleased to see her that I could almost feel tears building.

I stopped being emotional for long enough for her to answer.

"I'm collecting you! Everyone's heading to the restaurant for your surprise leaving do!" she answered, eagerly.

"SURPRISE!" belted in Amanda, from behind Alison.

"Amanda! I didn't even see you there! You're here! Are you okay? I missed you ... I ... I ... oh, come here!" I said, as I pulled her close for a hug.

When I released her from my death grip, I knew I had to straighten things out.

"I'm sorry, so sorry, for leaving you in a mess, with the flat and the bills and everything, I'll help you find a new flatmate and I've a cheque her for the rent and all the rest of it ... and ... yeah, I'm sorry," I repeated.

"You, Louise Casey, are the biggest eejit I have ever met! I don't care about all that shite, I'm just happy to see you!" replied Amanda, beaming.

"Why were you so weird with me on the phone the last day then? I thought you were angry with me, not that I blame you," I quickly added.

"I was ... busy. That's all, you silly moo. Don't worry about the flat and everything else, I've already got someone lined up to move in next week," she answered, with a suspicious twinkle in her eye.

"Who?" I asked.

"Never mind that, what are you going to wear? We're going dancing afterwards, no objections! Alison's booked us a VIP booth at Vanity, because she is a genius," Amanda informed.

"Ah no, sure you got in touch with everyone and sorted the restaurant and everything, I did nothing!" shushed Alison.

Impressed as I was at Alison booking the booth at what was Dublin's best nightclub, I was more intrigued by how my two best friends were interacting.

Was this sarcasm? Or were they, dare I say? Being nice to each other? Miracles do happen it seems.

My packing was halted, and the girls suggested and discarded ninety percent of my wardrobe. Then Alison unpacked most of my bags until she found a dress that I had bought a year previously, BB (Before Breakdown): a strapless black chiffon number, which dipped long at the back and short the front. My hair went up, down, then up again after being GHD'd to within an inch of its life. I did my makeup, and after one or two (four) glasses of wine for the road, we set off to the restaurant.

It felt like old times again, getting dressed up and going out with the girls. I began to wonder if I was making the right decision, moving home. I would miss this lifestyle so much. My *independence* was something I planned to cling to and I already had arranged to view flats to rent close to the shop so I wouldn't be living with my parents for the rest of my life. Slightly tipsy, I began to feel nostalgic for the carefree party filled life I had lost. Melancholy threatened to dampen my spirits, alarmed by my sudden change of mood, I shook my head and mentally shook myself.

I will have a new life, a better, healthier life. I *will* be happy and successful, and I can still go out, it would just mean another train journey is all.

We arrived at the restaurant after a mercifully short walk in our heels. I then began to wonder what Amanda meant by "everyone" heading to the restaurant?

I then spotted our table and my question was answered. Mikhal and Mrs Upstairs sat side by side and I was convinced they were holding hands under the table.

Tony waved over at Alison who confusedly furrowed her brow.

"What the fuck is he doing here?" She asked nobody in particular.

"Alison!" Tony called across the restaurant, causing other diners to look around at him.

"Oh my god, he's going to make a show of us," muttered Alison, hiding her face, I could see the excitement in her eyes though.

"Alison, I was an eejit, a gobshite! A fool! A complete and utter tosser! I love you, and our baby, and I miss you so much! Can you forgive me? I promise I'll make it up to you; I'll do all the night feeds and the nappies! I'll even ... I'll clean the cats litter tray forever! Please, Al, I'm desperate!" he called, still on the other side of the restaurant.

Alison had come out from behind me, I felt her hesitate, her hand cupping her small bump absently, she nibbled her lip, and then seemed to decide.

"What about the divorce papers? I got them this morning! You changed your tune!" she said, accusingly, with hurt in her eyes.

"I know," he said, clearly ashamed. "I applied ages ago, I'd almost forgotten about it until this morning, it made me realise how much of an eejit I've been," he said, clearly riddled with guilt.

"You big thick gobshite! I love you, too! And I'll hold you to that!" she shouted back.

Tony then half ran, half shuffled his way through all the tables until he reached Alison.

"I mean it, babe," he said, softly, quieter now, this was clearly meant for just the two of them. I looked away, but still heard.

"I love you more than life itself, Al, I was scared, and freaked out by all the responsibility, and I was selfish and stupid, but I know now, this is where I'm meant to be, with you, and the bump," he chuckled.

Alison replied, "Alright, Jesus, don't get so American about it." I looked back and saw her smile, then reach into her bag and retrieve her wedding ring. Tony took it from her, and then gently placed it on her finger. The whole restaurant applauded, it was like something from a rom-com, and I, along with half the restaurant, cheered and cried a little in happiness for them.

After Tony and Alison had finished kissing, like a pair of teenagers, they regained their composure and their sense of Irish shame at being caught snogging in public. They looked so happy to be reunited. Of course, they would have a lot ahead of them, healing the wounds that separation had caused, but just looking at them, you just knew that they would sort it.

If I had thought that would be the only shock of the night, I was mistaken.

When we reached our table, I found Colm seated there, who then greeted Amanda with a quick but firm kiss.

I decided to say nothing, as I knew how embarrassed he would get, but I had a feeling who Amanda's new roommate would be.

Also at the table was Mam, Dad, my sister, Brian, and Laura.

"What are you all doing here? Did you drive up? You let me get the train for no reason! You bastards!" I laughed, good naturedly.

"Brian drove," answered Dad, already looking a bit glassy-eyed.

"We thought we would surprise you, to celebrate how ... well you are!" Man chipped in. "And the shopping up here is only brilliant, how come you never said?" she scolded.

I caught my sister rolling my eyes and winked conspiratorially at her.

After our starters, which took ages as the conversation was flowing so well, I decided to go get some fresh air, I was also out of cigarettes and took my opportunity to run to the off license at the end of the street. How well everyone was getting on surprised me as it was such an odd mixture of people. Mam, Dad, Mikhal, and Mrs Upstairs got on famously and we're already making hiccupy plans to visit for weekends.

"I'll be back in a minute, just need to run and get fags," I told the table, who all seemed to be too wrapped up in conversations and staring into each other's eyes to notice. The happiness and warmth at that table was palpable, and heartwarming.

Laura, my comrade in singleton arms, offered to come with me.

"Not at all, stay in the warm, I'll only be a minute," I waved her off.

Out on the street, the air hit me and I realised how tipsy I was, I liked it, I decided. I walked through the Friday night party crowd peaceably, more at ease in such a crowd than I had been in months. I nosily looked through the shop windows as I passed. I passed another restaurant, one that was famous for having poor hygiene and a cheap menu, thinking about the lovely main course that was waiting for me in the restaurant, I hurried on until I noticed a familiar face.

Kevin. He was sitting at a table by the window, alone. I considered waving to him, alerting him to my presence, but I decided to just study him for a moment. He looked so serious, sketchy almost. He looked over his shoulder and motioned to someone that I couldn't see. I wish it had stayed that way because when I did see him I lost a life.

Kevin and Muggerman sat together at their table, and engaged in what looked like a low, muttered conversation. I stayed in my post at the window, hidden by an outdoor smoking parasol. Kevin reached into his pocket and produced what looked like money, he swapped it with Man Fucker for a small carrier bag that I knew, I just *knew* contained my purse and phone.

Strangely enough, my first thought was "where's the rest of it?"

I stepped away from the window. Terror and betrayal loomed in on me, trying to shut me down, to transform me into the wreck of a person I had recovered from.

My mind raced what should I do? Should I scream blue murder and alert everyone in the street? I really wanted to go into the restaurant and kick the living daylights out of both of them, because my fear was starting to be replaced with anger. Should I call the Guards and ... wait ... I knew exactly what to do.

I turned back and quickly returned to our table in the restaurant.

The concierge fetched him for me and after a brief conversation, Colm went off to catch his first bad guy. I watched him leave with pride, like a mothers on her child's first day at school, wanting to go after him and tie his shoelaces, which actually were untied.

I rejoined the table, and when Amanda asked about Colm, I told her that he had gone to take a call from work. Not entirely a lie to be fair. It was just that the evening had been so perfect; I refused to sully it by talking about Kevin and his pal. When Colm returned thirty minutes later, I watched him cross the room in anticipation, my heart in my chest, had he done it? Had he caught them? A double thumbs up gave me the answer I needed. Amanda seemed to realise something was up and started to ask, but Colm smoothly kissed her and said he would tell her later. He had a new air of confidence about him, like he was on cloud nine.

After a while, everyone seemed to accept that we weren't telling, so they carried on with the evening, nobody could ignore how elated I was though, for the first time in months, I felt safe. Our meal lasted for hours, course after delicious course. The real special that evening was, of course, being surrounded by friends and family.

After the restaurant, we all carried on to the nightclub, where we were treated like royalty. Mam and Dad in a trendy place like Vanity, trying to blend in was hysterical, even more so when they danced. It was the best night of life so far. As we all danced in a big circle, I felt myself being twirled by everyone and falling into different arms every time, always being caught. I would never be the same person as before, but maybe this was better, I realised how much I had changed and felt empowered, then I danced and danced all night, like a superwoman.